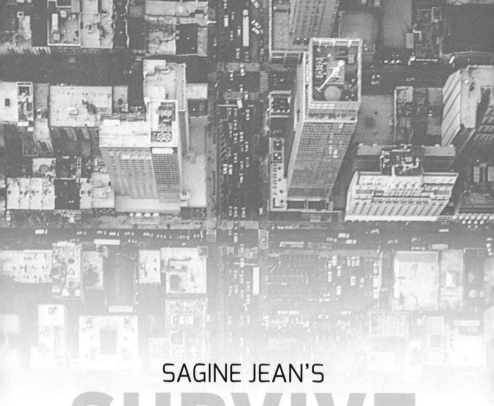

SAGINE JEAN'S

# SURVIVE

# DARKNESS

**EPIC**
Escape

An Imprint of EPIC Press
EPICPRESS.COM

# Darkness
## Survive

Written by Sagine Jean

Copyright © 2018 by Abdo Consulting Group, Inc.

Published by EPIC Press™
PO Box 398166
Minneapolis, MN 55439

Printed in the United States of America.

Cover design by Christina Doffing
Images for cover art obtained from iStockPhoto.com
Edited by Rue Moran

LIBRARY OF CONGRESS CATALOGING-IN-PUBLICATION DATA
Names: Jean, Sagine, author.
Title: Darkness / by Sagine Jean.
Description: Minneapolis, MN : EPIC Press, 2018. | Series: Survive
Summary: Two teens, high school senior Sydney and rookie cop Will, must work together to
    find Sydney's autistic younger brother. But the most violent hurricane in New York's history
    leaves them stranded in a labyrinth of subway tunnels.
Identifiers: LCCN 2016962939 | ISBN 9781680767315 (lib. bdg.)
    | ISBN 9781680767872 (ebook)
Subjects: LCSH: Disasters—Fiction. | Missing children—Fiction. | Survival—Fiction.
    | Adventure and adventurers—Fiction. | Young adult fiction.
Classification: DDC [Fic]—dc23
LC record available at http://lccn.loc.gov/2016962939

EPIC
Press

EPICPRESS.COM

*To Mom, Dad, and Marven, for
giving me the courage to dream*

# CHAPTER 1

*Sydney*

**B**EFORE MY FATHER LEFT US FOR HIS SECRE-tary, he told me three words I'll never forget. And no, they weren't "I love you." The man would rather choke on his own blood than get sentimen-tal—which I guess makes two of us.

And besides, a simple, generic "I love you" would never have helped as much as what he really said. He had kneeled down so he could look me in the eyes. "When you look someone in the eyes," he always said, "they can't just pretend that they never heard you." I'd wanted to look away, but he held my chin tightly in his grip and watched me as I squirmed.

"Stay tough, Syd." That'd been it. He'd torn my life apart, and that was the closest thing to an apology I'd ever get. And, well, I took it. I held on to it the way little kids hold on to blankets and grown men to booze because "Stay tough, Syd" was everything. "Stay tough, Syd" was a promise, an omen, a war cry in the dark. It meant protect your brother, watch out for your mom, be the tough one. "Stay tough, Syd," meant that I was strong, that I'd always been strong, and the only way to deal with all the crap that my dad and the world were going to throw at me was to stay that way.

So that's what I did.

I took my father's advice, and when he walked out, I slammed the door in his face and didn't look back. Not once.

- - -

The rain started at about nine a.m. and didn't let up until a quarter past five. Even now, the city is soaked in the kind of heavy wet air that only comes before a storm. Since the weekend, everyone on the news has been saying it's going to be a big one—bigger than Hurricane Sandy had been. They keep saying, "Stay in your homes. Only leave if your mom's in the hospital or the old lady who lives downstairs tries to set your building on fire again"—serious stuff like that.

But trying to tell New Yorkers to stay home is like trying to tell God not to raise the sun in the morning—both are too stubborn to listen. Outside my window, I can already see people shaking off rain from their umbrellas and resuming dinner plans that they probably only canceled this morning. People and cars fly past my street, lighting up the evening in streaks and blurs of color, dancing over puddles and water droplets. Looking at everyone now, you would never know that it rained a whole ocean in about a day's time. But what little is left of the sun is out now, and New Yorkers wouldn't be New Yorkers if they didn't take advantage of opportunities.

"Sydney, are you even listening?" I look back at

my phone, shocked to find it in my hand and the screen lighting up with the name "Ezra." No, I hadn't been. I'd completely forgotten that I was on the phone, let alone in the middle of a conversation with my boyfriend.

I turn away from my window.

"Yeah, yeah, course. Something about the band, right?"

"Of course something about the band! Damn it, Sydney, you promised. You looked me in the eye and you said 'Ezra, I'll be there.' Sydney, it's our first paying gig!"

"Ezra, the hurricane warning . . . "

"What hurricane? Half the city is out tonight; check the news again. There is no storm; those jerks got it wrong."

I tilt the phone away and groan loudly into my pillow.

Ezra's not like me. He's only about a year or two older but he's the kind of guy that grew up in some swanky sheltered neighborhood in downtown

Brooklyn, with a lawyer dad and a doctor mom. He's got more money than Ma, Sammy, or I'd know what to do with. Instead of . . . I don't know . . . going to college or something, Ezra spends his allowance on four-hundred-dollar leather pants and bribing clubs and cafés to let him and his mediocre band play. He says it's the price for exposure. I just think it's an excuse not to spend any time actually getting good.

"Sydney, this isn't just some rehearsal you can show up to whenever you feel like it. This is the rest of my life!" I try not to roll my eyes as I get out of bed and put on a raincoat—because well, you never know.

"I'll be there, I just have to take Sammy with me. My mom's asleep so . . . "

"Honestly, Sydney, you are the most selfish person I've ever met."

I can picture him now, dark hair gelled back and a pout on his face that threatens to disrupt the careful makeup he's just applied. I lean against the doorframe to my bedroom, delighting a little in being another couple minutes late.

"And who are you," I ask, "Mother Teresa?"

It'd be a waste of both my time and his if I have to explain to him why I won't be on time, and lately picking fights with Ezra is easier—and frankly more fun—than actually talking to him.

"Just be there, okay? Let your mom take care of Sammy for once."

I pause for a moment, half out the door of my room, wondering if I'd imagined the edge of concern in his voice.

"It's not that easy. She's got work in the morning and—"

"I don't care, Sydney. Things can't be all about you! What about my life? All you worry about is your stupid kid brother!"

If I could reach through the phone and kick him in the face, I would.

"Hey look, the last place I want to be is in Midtown, cheering you on like some—"

He's already hung up and I'm sure I've screamed loud enough to wake up both my mom and Sammy from their naps.

Sure enough, Sam comes padding out of his room in a rumpled T-shirt and shorts. "Syd?" he says, his voice a little croaky from sleep.

"Hey, Sammy-jams. Wanna go get dressed? I'll take you over to Kathy's." Kathy is one of the few people I'm close to. She is nice and I trust her enough to leave her alone with Sammy.

Sammy rubs sleep from his eyes with a chubby little fist. He's got dad's blue eyes, so it's always a little hard to look at him at first—too many reminders. But I'm getting used to it.

"Why can't I stay here? With you and mom?" He's cranky; he hates being woken up from naps. It messes up the carefully organized routine he's used to. Sammy likes schedules, and any little disruption can send him into full panic mode. I open up my arms and he steps into them like he's done a thousand times before. I'm the only person he lets hug

11

him like this, so it makes me squeeze him a little tighter. Even though he's seven now, he still smells like a baby—all talcum powder and dewy skin.

"Sorry bud, I'm going out. And, well, Mom's . . . You know how she is in the afternoon. Especially when she's got back-to-back shifts in the hospital."

He nods, and I can see how sad he is. He's probably thinking about how other kids don't need babysitters when their moms are at home. He's probably thinking about Dad, and why he doesn't have one. Or maybe me, and wondering why I'm such a screw-up. Hell, who knows what Sammy's ever thinking. His blue eyes are too sharp for a seven year old, and I swear they hide galaxies behind them.

The hug seems to do the trick for the moment, and he's calm enough that he doesn't make too much of a fuss when I make him pack up his stuff and head out the door.

"Did you know that some species of bird don't let their chicks leave the nest until they're fully adults?"

Sammy says, rhythmically squeezing my hand to the beat of some unheard song.

"No Sams, I didn't," I say absentmindedly, as I pull him through a throng of people. It's getting dark out and the air outside is still heavy and wet, but lower Manhattan is as crowded as it would be on a sunny summer day. Even with the supposed storm of the century lurking on the horizon of this night, everyone and their mother seems to be clamoring to get inside the Fourteenth Street station. It takes everything in me not to flip the bird to a guy that nearly knocks Sammy and me off the stairs.

"It's because they have a greater chance of survival once they reach full maturity," Sammy says, tugging on my rain jacket until I have no choice but to turn away from the turnstile and look at him.

While I look like my mother—Puerto Rican and all curves—Sammy is blue-eyed and blond just like my dad. Still, he's nothing like the man that left us when he was just a baby. Sammy lives on facts and truths about the world that you can only find in textbooks and nature documentaries. And even though he'll never convey emotion by saying he's sad, happy, or wishes that he saw our mom more often, you can always tell what he's feeling through the facts he lets you in on. The more persistent he is about them, the more agitated he usually is.

"Listen Sammy," I say, putting a hand on his shoulder. "I can drop you off at Kathy's, or you can come with me. It's only one hour, and you know if mom could take a night off to spend with you she would, but she's gotta work."

He looks at me, his steely blue eyes turning my question over in his mind.

"Kathy talks too much," he says, and that's that. I stifle the urge to laugh. Kathy and I have been friends since we were little. We aren't terribly close but I trust her, even with Sammy. The kid is right, though. She could talk forever.

"Alright, then. We're only gonna be at the concert for an hour. You can play on my phone the whole time and put in your earplugs if it gets too loud. Or close your eyes, even. But right now you gotta give me your hand, babe, our train's coming."

Finally he agrees and we board the F train toward Sixty-Third for Ezra's concert. I swear this boy must owe me a fortune for all the metro cards I've spent hauling my butt uptown for him.

The rain starts falling again in light drizzles as Sammy and I climb out of the subway. The train took a little longer than usual to get us here, but we're only about ten minutes late. We should be fine . . . I hope.

Thick drops cling to my jacket and hair as I pull Sammy toward Sixtieth Street and the Avalon Café, where Ezra and his band are performing.

"Did you know that your chance of dying increases when you go out past eight?" says Sammy, and I sigh. Jeez, for a seven-year-old, the kid is more morbid than an old lady in hospice.

"I know you want to go home, Sams. Alright? We'll be out in an—" I start, but my phone buzzes and I look down to see all the texts I've missed since we've been underground. Ugh. Curse subways and their lack of cell service.

Glad you're actually coming this time.

Get here soon.

Hurry! You're gonna miss my set!

Come. NOW!!!!

What the hell Sydney?? Where are you???

All five delayed texts are from Ezra. Finally my phone chimes again, revealing another final text from Ezra that I missed.

Don't even bother coming. I'm done.

My brain's telling me that it's just Ezra being dramatic as usual, but my heart is racing. He's done? His set is five songs long—he shouldn't be done this quickly. Unless . . . unless he's not talking about his set. Unless he's talking about us.

My heart skips a beat.

I've dated Ezra for almost a year now and never has he told me to not bother coming to one of his gigs. I run my hands through my hair in frustration. It hasn't always been like this. Ezra used to make me laugh; he used to make me lie in my bed at night and dream about all the things I wanted to say to him the next time we met. I liked that we were different; I liked that his world was full of music and four hundred-dollar pants and worry-free thoughts. No kid brothers, working moms, and absentee dads. He didn't have to stay tough for anyone. Most importantly, I didn't have to stay tough for him.

I race toward Sixtieth, Sammy in tow, flying through the rain with my dark hair tumbling behind me.

I get to Avalon and see that Ezra was right. His set is over. I watch through the windows as his bandmates pack up, putting guitars back in their cases, turning off amps. I take a step toward the door when finally I see her. Perky and pretty with long red hair and flawless skin. I see Ezra, off to the side, whispering in her ear, letting his band do all the grunt work.

I should stop this. I should run in and say something, but it's too late. He pulls her hips close to his and kisses her, and not like they just met. Like they've done it once and again and a thousand times before.

And as I watch him cheat on me in this cafe, I realize that we were doomed from the start—even before this kiss. He's always been selfish. That was why things between us weren't like they used to be. Because Ezra is worry-free, careless, and he spends four hundred dollars on leather pants and kisses other girls when his girlfriend doesn't come at his beck and call.

I should be relieved—and I guess a part of me is. The end of Ezra and me has been coming for weeks, months even. This just cements things.

Relief isn't the emotion that swells inside of me as I see Ezra's hands on this girl. It's rage that's pouring into me, lighting me up and making me want to scream and tear him apart limb from limb.

This dude just stepped out on the wrong girl.

I'm ready to yank the door to the cafe open when I hear Sammy at my side.

"Did you know that if kids go to bed by eight

they do better in school?" he asks, and I pull myself away from the door. I can't cause a scene with Sammy here. The commotion would be too much for him. He'd probably run away and hide.

"It's summer. School doesn't start for another three weeks," I grumble, pulling Sammy away from the cafe front. School—senior year, without a boyfriend to take to homecoming.

Without another word, I turn away from the door and walk back toward the station, anger still coursing through my veins. The rain comes down harder and the wind picks up almost as if to match my fury. Every moment that Ezra and I have ever shared flashes through my mind, good and bad, now ruined by the memory of him and the redhead.

*God, I could just kill him!*

The wind grows stronger and I imagine how I'm going to stomp him into the ground the next time I see him. How he's going to get his butt handed to him.

Sammy and I get to the station in record time,

swipe through the turnstile, and immediately find the F train waiting for us.

"Did you know the average hurricane spins at a velocity of seventy-four miles per hour?"

"Whatever, Sam!" I snap as we take our seats. Sammy doesn't even flinch. He never flinches. He just looks away from me and goes back to staring into space. I immediately want to hug him and apologize, but he wouldn't even get why I was sorry.

I sit in my seat and stew for a little, thinking about how I want to break Ezra's neck, until I notice the train hasn't moved. How it's been here at Sixty-Third for almost ten minutes, and still the doors have not closed and the train has not moved on to its next stop. I watch as the other passengers look at each other questioningly.

An automated train message comes on: "*Ladies and gentlemen, we are being held momentarily because of train traff—*"

The message starts but cuts and a human voice—the train conductor—comes on. "I'm sorry ladies and gentlemen, but the track is flooded and the F train will not be running today. I repeat: the F train will not be running today."

As if this day could get any worse.

And then I see the water, and it does. The conductor wasn't kidding. In fact, he may have even downplayed it. Water seeps onto the train from both the closed and open train doors, spilling onto sandy-colored linoleum floors like waves creeping up-shore.

I hear Sammy squeal beside me as everyone begins to leave the train in a strange sort of panic. It's just water, what can water really do to you? But this is a New York City subway train—it's late, it's unreliable, but never does it fill up with water.

"Sams, let's get out of here," I say. People come pouring out with us, and it's impossible not to feel a little disoriented. Two trains have been emptied during rush hour—this train and the one on the track next to us. That's more than a thousand people, easy. Not to mention the people waiting on the platform and those coming down the stairs who now have to turn back. The water isn't just seeping onto the train cars, it's spilling over the platform, creating waves and splashes as people run up the stairs and toward turnstile exits. It's the storm that everyone—even the weathermen themselves—thought wasn't coming, reaching us at full force.

It's chaos with the water surging higher and higher as people shove toward the stairs. The exodus of people causes a traffic jam, and Sammy and I are at a standstill, caught behind a line of people with the same destination: out.

I hear Sammy's breathing get heavier. He hates crowds more than anything in the world. He hates when people push and prod at him. If it's only for a second, he can close his eyes and think of something else, but if it's like this—constant and nonstop—it's too much for him.

"Hang in there, Sammy," I say and make a move to hold him close to me, but he pushes away. If he can't even deal with me in his personal space, then he must really be agitated. Police officers appear almost out of nowhere to help usher us to safety, informing everyone which exits are closed or flooded shut and which ones we can use.

This storm is coming, and it's coming fast. I think about Ezra and how he'd said that the weatherman got it wrong, and I'm mad all over again.

"It's going to be okay, Sams. I prom—" I look down at my side.

He's not there. Sammy isn't here. I panic, then catch my breath when I see his bright purple raincoat weaving through the crowd, pushing past everyone and heading deeper into the subway.

"SAMMY!" I scream, but he's not listening, he's not turning back. I chase after him, my feet sloshing through the water on the platform. I scream his name again, but despite the water rushing in, the people trying to escape, and the sheer terror in my voice, he keeps going.

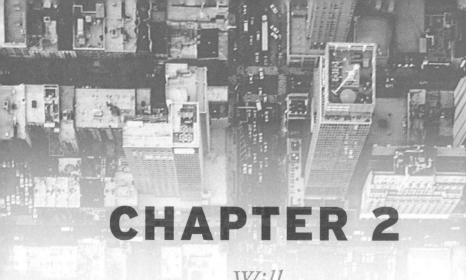

# CHAPTER 2

*Will*

**T**HERE'S SOMETHING ABOUT PUTTING ON A uniform that changes you. Well maybe not you, exactly, but the way everyone sees you. Suddenly, you're not the nerd from down the block with his nose in a book. You're not the kid who buys groceries for his mom at the deli. Suddenly, you're a man—no matter what you feel on the inside—and that's all that counts.

"You look so handsome," my mother says as she smooths the lapels out on the dark blue shirt. "My baby boy all grown up." She takes the lint roller from the table next to her and pushes it down my arms.

As if the cop uniform I've never worn a day in my life has been through the washer. "There you go, sweetheart," she says, her grin wider than I've seen in a long time. Too bad I know it'll be short-lived. "Doesn't Will look handsome, Bobby?" she asks the hunched-over form on the couch.

My father looks up from the TV to glare at me, his dark eyes filled with venom. He takes the butt of the cigarette out of his mouth and puts it out against the armchair. My mother winces, her smile gone.

He eyes my uniform, letting the cigarette smolder against the already ruined black leather.

He laughs, short and abrupt, and I put my hand on Ma's shoulder and try to make my eyes just as venomous as his, waiting for his next move.

But there is no next move. My father watches me in the yellowing light of the living room because that's all he can do now—watch and be bitter. He turns back to the TV and reaches for a beer can as I give my Ma's shoulder a light squeeze. She looks up at me, and I know she sees it, too, this blue uniform saving us.

- - -

To be honest, I'm nothing more than a glorified meter maid. I don't even get to drive the patrol car, let alone be in one unless Captain Gerri's feeling particularly less crabby and decides to give me a ride to the station, like she does this morning.

Even as I get into the cop car, I feel my mother's eyes on me all the way from the living room window. I can almost hear her voice chattering with her friends about it. "My Will's the youngest officer on the squad, you know. That boy's gonna shoot all the way to captain." I feel her pride on me like a weight and stand a little taller as I get in, just to help carry the load.

"Thanks for the ride, Ger," I say as we pull away from the curb. Raindrops from a coming storm hit the windshield as we leave my mother and the rest of my neighborhood behind.

"That's Captain to you," she says. "And it's only 'cause I knew your father back when he was captain. Don't go thinking you're special." Then a flash of a smile appears on her face before it disappears and her eyes settle on the road. Like everyone I work with, she knew my dad way back when he was captain of the precinct. She knew me, too, which is why it's probably a surprise to her and everyone else that I chose to be a cop instead of going to college.

"You ready for your first day, kid?" she asks, her voice roaring over the pattering of rain. Instead of answering, my eyes follow the windshield wipers as they move back and forth. They say we're supposed to get a hurricane today. My mom even shut down her salon so she could stay indoors. But I have the type of job that doesn't let you close shop just for a little rain.

"I graduated top of my class at the academy, Ger—Captain."

"That's not an answer to my question." She takes a sharp right and we're on the bridge, stuck behind cars and trucks all on their way to Manhattan. Apparently none of them watched the weather channel. Seeing how impatiently she jerks the wheel, I half expect her to put the sirens on just to beat the traffic. Then she does. The sirens flare on with a blast of light and sound and suddenly we're sailing across the bridge.

"Gerri, you can't . . . you can't just . . . " I start to protest, but it's pointless, the captain does what she wants just like she's always done.

"You still haven't answered my question," she says as we whoosh through the rain, other cars moving to the side so we can pass.

"I've been ready since I could walk. I just wish I wasn't handing out tickets today."

"We've all got to start somewhere." She shrugs.

I've known Gerri since I was just a kid. She was the lieutenant under my dad and had been over to my house more times than I could count. I knew her almost as well as I knew my mom—so I knew that she didn't just start somewhere. Gerri had been the youngest detective at her precinct, breaking city records.

"I got in this so I could protect people—do something. Everyone knows that meter maids are just jerks on a power trip."

"Watch your mouth, Will. Your father was a meter maid when he first started out and so was your father's father."

I don't want to tell her that she's proving my point, so I stay silent.

We get to the Fifty-third Precinct of Union Square within a half hour thanks to Gerri's illegal usage of the sirens, and I can't help but feel like I'm home. Most people would find the chaos of the downtown Manhattan department a little disarming, with officers either roughhousing and swearing in thick New York accents or running around getting ready to answer a distress call. The attitude in the room swings dramatically from urgency and control to laughter and camaraderie. I love it. This is the place I've been dreaming about since I was a kid; this is one of the reasons why I wanted to be a cop. I wanted this—the feeling of actually being a part of something that mattered, the feeling of being a part of a family.

"Welcome to the force, Kid," Gerri says at my side, her hand landing roughly on my shoulders. "Glad to have you." She smiles. Other cops don't really notice, but the few who do and remember who I am give me nods and warm claps on the back, and I feel more accomplished than I've ever felt—more real somehow.

"Ready to get to some action?" Gerri asks and I nod eagerly, thinking maybe something's happened. Maybe I won't be a meter maid today after all.

Then she puts a ticket pad in my hand and I immediately deflate. When Gerri sees my expression, she merely laughs and moves on to look at the rest of the officers. She goes on to talk about the upcoming storm and protocol, but I duck out toward the back, my fingers shaking with energy. *This is it. This is the first day of the rest of my life*, I say to myself urgently enough that I hope it'll stop feeling like a dream.

"Officer," Gerri yells at me, "get to your post. Those tickets aren't going to hand themselves out."

- - -

The best thing about my job is that I get to drive around in a meter maid wagon. It also happens to be the worst. On one hand, the privacy of the one-person vehicle is comparable to none; on the other, nearly everyone who sees me coming knows I'm not a real cop. Well, I guess you can't have it all.

"Are you talking to me?" asks a hairy man in his forties with a thick New York accent.

"Sir, if you'd just—"

"Are *you* talking to *me*?" His voice takes on an edge that says that I'd be on the ground right now if it weren't for my uniform, but also an edge that says he'd probably put me on the ground anyway.

"If this is your blue Toyota in a handicap spot, then yes, I am," I say evenly, remembering my training, even though it doesn't really apply much here. Then again, this guy looks like he's about to stab me in the stomach.

"That's a joke. A skinny little meter maid telling me when and where I can't park. You got some nerve, kid. You know I could kick the crap out of you, right?"

"So could I, but way before you could even lift a finger," I say, straight-faced. "And then slap you with about a dozen citations and charges, including attempted assault on a police officer." The man's face sours and he crosses his arms, accepting his ticket with little more than a grunt and an eye roll.

"Screw you and your stupid little meter wagon," he yells as he gets in his car.

"Good day to you, too," I mumble as I watch him drive away. It's been more than six hours—an entire day of getting yelled and cursed at by hairy Italians and mean New Yorkers. If I wanted this, I would have just stayed home today.

I hear thunder in the distance and the crackle of lightning as wind whooshes through my hair. It's rained hard all day, with Hurricane Angelica looming over the horizon, projected to reach land by tonight. Then for a little while, around early evening, everything quieted. The world stilled and the sun came out, just for a moment, and the city became roaring and bustling again. Now the rain is settling back in, pounding against the city as if it never left, and I can see people racing back to buildings and subway stations. I wonder for a moment if I should be worried when the radio in my meter maid wagon roars to life with a crackle of static and electricity.

*"I need all available units in the Lexington Ave and Sixty-Third Street area to head to the subway. I repeat, all available units are needed to help evacuate the station."* Clear instructions and protocols follow and I listen in rapt attention.

My heart skips in my chest and my fingers leap

toward the walkie-talkie at my shoulder. "Copy. This is Officer Will Tatum, heading there now."

My fingers shake as I plug my key in the wagon, heading toward the subway station on Sixty-Third and Lexington with an excitement I can't quite hide. This is nothing really—just a call to escort commuters safely out of a flooding station. Just routine stuff for a storm. But it's something that actually matters. It's not protecting laws that mostly exist to make the city money. It's not ruining someone's day with a fine. It's looking out for people, helping someone in need. And as cliché as it sounds, it's another reason why I pushed myself through the academy.

I step out of the vehicle at Sixty-Third and zip my police-issued rain jacket as high as it will go. The rain is falling in torrents now. It was the lightest of drizzles only thirty minutes ago. By the time I get underground, I'm soaked—the humidity of the stagnant, recycled air the only thing keeping me from shivering.

Though the storm isn't what's important right

now. There's chaos all around me. People running to and fro, careening into each other, all pressing toward the exits. All the while, water pours in from the ceiling as though faucets have been turned on.

I relay the instructions from the call just as fluidly as I learned in the academy: voice authoritative and sure, and stance firm and unrelenting as I direct them toward the safest exit.

Then again, this is New York, and nothing is ever as easy as protocol and the academy made it out to be. This is a big station with multiple exits that lead to different streets, passageways, and avenues, and everyone is keen on getting home as quickly as possible. So no one listens to us as we shout directions to go toward a designated exit. No one listens as we try to usher them against the rising water.

When you're a cop, you have to keep your cool no matter what the situation. It's one of the first things you learn. But it's almost impossible here with the commotion, the people, and the surge of water almost past the top of my boots.

I move through the crowd trying to get to the stragglers—the couple of people going the opposite direction, still trying to get to their damn exits. Remarkably, no one sees me as a meter maid here. They all listen with a staunch "Yes, officer." A feeling of pride swells through the commotion in my chest.

I see one girl running, water splashing in her wake, and I move to catch up to her, grabbing a gentle hold of her elbow.

"If you'd please take the designated exit, miss." I repeat the orders to her—a teenage girl, dark-haired, olive-toned, and pretty. Yet there's something off about her. For one, she doesn't reply with a quick "Yes." Her lips are set in an angry scowl, she stares at me with defiance, her honey-colored eyes clearly unafraid of authority.

"Miss, if you'd please." She's maybe seventeen, but she holds herself like she's older, like she knows better, and everything about it unnerves me. She continues to stare at me and I'm about to repeat myself sternly when she opens her mouth to speak.

"My brother is missing."

I blink at her.

"Well if you'd just follow me toward the exit, I'm sure we can get to the station before the storm fully hits and file a—"

"No," she says insistently. "Here! He's missing here. He ran away and I need to find him now. So please, you have to let me go get him."

I almost don't know what to do. Past the defiance, past the anger is something I know all too well—fear. But there are rules, protocols, and procedures that have to be followed.

"I'm afraid I can't let you go farther through the system, miss. If you want to find him, we'll just have to call a rescue team down here once the space clears."

"And the storm ends? That will take hours! I don't have hours, I have to start looking now. He's getting farther away!"

The desperation in her voice, the tears threatening to spill from her eyes, is enough to make the me outside this uniform give her anything she wants. But here, on the job? I'm not the same Will—I can't be. Maybe she sees the apology on my face, the reluctance, because before I can say a word, she slips out of my grasp and runs farther into the flooding subway.

"Wait!" I yell, but despite how loud and authoritative I try to sound, she keeps going. I have no choice but to run after her.

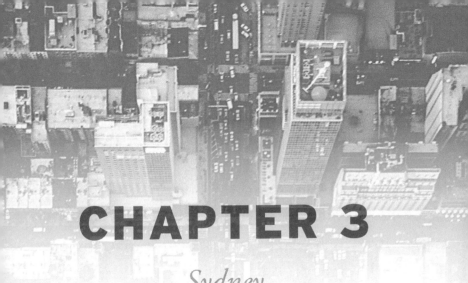

# CHAPTER 3

## *Sydney*

**T**HERE AND GONE. ONE MOMENT. JUST ONE moment and already his purple jacket is not even a spot in the distance. I'm running through murky green water with a cop on my back shouting for me to stop, but I'm too frantic. Too startled, too afraid to even register that I might be breaking the law. Still, it's Sammy—my Sammy, my little brother. And this is all my fault.

He could die and it'd be all my fault.

The crowd thins as I keep running and I know I'm past the point of no return. Passageways toward different train lines pop out at me and I try to pretend I'm Sammy. Think like him, get inside his mind.

Sammy has Asperger's, a form of autism that can make social interactions about the worst thing in the world for him

It's why he hates crowds, people touching him, why he only drinks from a red water bottle, and communicates difficult-to-process emotions through random facts. He favors things on the right side, so I take every right turn. He hates noise, so I take the routes that are the most silent.

"Stop right there, miss! Stop!" The cop keeps screaming, but I barely have time to register him. The water surges up my calf, but I don't stop. I have to find Sammy. I need to find him. Still—I need to lose this cop first.

Sammy likes small spaces, so I know that finding him won't be easy. Luckily, it's also the perfect way to go where this cop won't follow. I veer away from a passageway leading toward a shuttle and move toward the tracks of the F train.

I can almost feel the officer's shock pulsing through the air as I do the unthinkable.

I run hard until I've gathered enough momentum to leap off of the ground and onto the subway tracks. Water splashes around me and I pray to whoever is listening that the electricity has been shut off because of the storm.

"Are you insane?" I hear him scream behind me. His voice breaks, its booming authority turning into something fearful and frantic.

*Good, don't follow me.* And not just because I know he'll try to take me back, but because the only person who should be doing something as reckless as jumping down to train tracks to save Sammy is me.

Then there's a second splash of water and a bright white flashlight shoots on. He's followed me—that stupid cop is following me.

"Get back here, miss! You're going to get yourself killed." His voice returns to an authoritative shout. He sounds almost unfeeling, his tone completely free of any trace of the previous fear. He doesn't even sound sympathetic, as if the fact that my little brother is off somewhere in this dark and flooded underground tunnel is something he doesn't care about. Something he won't even pretend to care about.

I feel anger boiling in my blood, rising with each water-soaked step I take, propelling me deeper and deeper into the tunnel. The water is only an inch or two past my ankles, but it's rising steadily as rainwater continues to leak from the concrete ceiling. My heart is still seizing in my chest when I finally I see it—just the type of exit Sammy would take, if I'm right and he's jumped on the tracks. A slightly open door, just shorter than my five-foot-three frame, appears on the right, and no matter how convoluted this all is, I know I've made the right choice. Sammy thinks like this—complicated and in tangents: every right turn, the small enclosed track tunnels, the tiny door on the right side in the tiny enclosed tunnel.

This has to work. I have to be right.

I fake a left turn just swiftly enough to make the

cop think I'm about to turn, but then I leap for the door and almost smile as I hear the cop fumble in my wake.

I must be the only one who was an all-star on the JV girls basketball team in middle school.

I try not to get too cocky as I press toward the door, my fingers latching onto the handle, and I'm suddenly jerked back by a hand on my raincoat.

I don't think. My body is a roll of nerves and energy that can't possibly be contained, even by some disgruntled cop.

So I don't hesitate; I don't think about future consequences or anything as practical as that. I just do.

All at once my limbs explode and I kick him hard in the stomach. My arms follow suit, and I push at his shoulders until he loses his balance.

With a grunt, he stumbles back into the water on the tracks and I keep moving, thoughts of Sammy, alone and shivering somewhere, clouding my mind.

*I'm coming, Sams. Don't worry I'm coming.*

I yank open the door and find a long, twisting staircase. I pull up the flashlight app on my iPhone and begin my descent. The farther down I go, the more my thoughts spiral. The cop lying in the water, the storm raging around us, Sammy lost to me forever.

He'd once told me that I was like a rock in the middle of an ocean. It was a rare moment of self-reflection that had made me hug him hard until he yelped and pushed me away from him. He didn't have to explain what he meant—I already knew. The world for Sammy was like a shifting current. Things moved too fast for him and too slow all at once. He could never find the right momentum or ever catch a break, but I was his rock. I stayed solid for him and immobile even when things got tough.

But I'd been too busy thinking of Ezra and our breakup to notice how agitated he'd been. I'd failed as his big sister, as his rock in the middle of a torrential sea.

And that blooming thought of failure pulses

through me as I reach the bottom of the staircase and see nothing there. A storage room, just an empty storage room with metal shelves filled with nothing.

Still, I ransack the room until the metal shelves dig into my skin and leave scratches. I call his name and the only voice that echoes in my ears is my own. I run up the stairs, through the darkness and out the door, running my shaking hands through my hair. My thoughts shift to the cop. Maybe he can help. Maybe if he sees how shaken, how close to breaking apart I am. Or maybe if I beg, beg until my voice goes hoarse and I run out of words.

But the cop isn't there. I pushed him—*kicked* him—into the water and he hasn't gotten up. He hasn't chased after me. Suddenly, a different panic takes hold of me.

I just hit a cop. And possibly knocked him unconscious. What is that . . . like thirty years in prison? I'm screwed. I'm so unbelievably screwed.

And what if he's injured, what if he's dead— drowned in the dark water? What if he has a wife and kids? People who depend on him, love him, and need him? What if I've just ruined all their lives just to find Sammy?

I search through the water, which has gotten much deeper since I ran through that door. My eyes strain in the white light of my phone, searching for movement. I almost frantically jump in myself when a hand claps me hard on the shoulder.

I freeze before turning to look at the angry police officer.

# CHAPTER 4

*Will*

**W**ATER. STINGING MY EYES, POURING IN MY throat, holding me in place. It almost feels tranquil, not at all like the panicky frantic feeling you get when you think that you're drowning. The darkness is like a comforter and the water is strangely warm, and I'm reminded of weekend mornings when I'd run into my parents' bed and hide under their covers. Back before my dad's injury, back when my family was a family.

That listless open feeling only lasts for a moment before I feel the static-y crackle of my radio going dead at my shoulder, until I feel my gun digging into my hip, my cap drifting off into the water. I swim forward and break the surface, my eyes scanning the tracks for any sign of the girl that pushed me in. For someone so small, she was much, *much* stronger than she looked. My stomach still aches from where she kicked me.

I know I should feel angry—I should be livid. I should be looking for her and locking her up in handcuffs so I can bring her back to the surface. After all, she did refuse an order from a police officer and she did kick me. Everything I've learned from the academy tells me that I should be trying to lock her up. But somehow, I don't want to. Somehow, I'm not angry.

She'd looked so desperate and afraid. As if her entire world had crumbled apart. Still, I have to find her. Not because I want to lock her up, but because what kind of person would I be if I left her here, in this dark, wet tunnel under the ground?

I hoist myself out of the water and onto the thin platform, obviously not meant for anyone to stand on. Suddenly, I see her. I must have floated a little ways up the track because she's behind me now. leaning so far toward the water it looks like she might fall in. She's looking for me, I realize—or at least I think she is.

I walk toward her, careful not to make any noise, then place my hand on her shoulder. She freezes, then whips around so fast we almost both lose our balance and go tumbling into the water.

"Don't touch me!" she yells and I move away, but I keep a hard stare fixed on her. Better for her to think I'm angry, better for her to not forget who's in charge of this situation. Though I'm having trouble remembering it myself.

"I'm not, but you can't run away from me again," I say evenly. She nods, her long, dark hair falling in her eyes, her stubborn jaw fixed in place.

"My name's Officer Will Tatum and I'm not here to hurt you, but we've got to get back. This place is like a powder keg about to explode. With the amount of rain falling, I'm surprised it's not completely submerged."

"My brother . . . " Her voice breaks.

"We'll send a rescue team down here as soon as we can. You can't sacrifice yourself trying to save him." Her gaze becomes defiant once again and I make my features just as hard. She's got to listen. We can't stay down here for much longer.

"You're a cop. Isn't that your job? To sacrifice yourself to save people?" Her questions make me uneasy. They make me want to fidget and find something to do with my hands, but I stand even straighter.

"It's also my job to follow orders and keep as many people safe as possible. I won't risk someone dying on some futile mission to find someone when we have no idea where they're hiding."

She shoves against my chest, anger clouding her features. "What kind of cop are you?" she says with disgust. I match her tone exactly.

"The kind that's gonna choose to look the other

way on both counts of you assaulting a police officer." *And the kind that's going to save your life,* I think to myself.

"I don't care!" she yells, and her voice echoes around us. "Get me in trouble! I dare you! But I will find my brother and you will not stop me."

"Miss—" Before I can reason with her anymore, the ground beneath of us begins to shake. Just slightly. Just the smallest of tremors. You wouldn't even notice if you weren't paying attention. But I am. A part of being a cop means knowing your surroundings. Understanding where you are and what may happen at all times.

I feel it before I hear it. That whooshing sound is almost soothing and gentle, like the sound you hear in a seashell. A poor, barely there imitation of a beach.

Suddenly, I know. The world seems to freeze, and there's barely enough time to grab the girl next to me when the largest body of water I've ever seen begins making its way down the tunnel. The girl isn't looking. She's still livid and trying to argue with me, her eyes lighting in sudden surprise as I grab her. Then she turns and sees what I see—the ten-foot-high surge of water coming toward us.

It's what I've feared since I first followed her here—that something would break at some higher level and submerge us in thousands of gallons of dirty water. That we would drown here and no one would ever know where to look for us. Her hand trembles in mine, just slightly, as though even here, at this split second, as our lives are on the line, she's trying hard not to show how afraid she is.

I don't think. I just act. With the water only yards away, I run toward the door that she just went through only moments before and shove us both inside. I put up my hands to seal the rust-covered door and push with all my might. The girl joins in too, just as the surge of water comes our way and nearly knocks me off my feet. But the door holds and I release a breath.

We stand there, on the staircase leading to God

knows where, behind a door blocking water, and God knows what else. We look at each other and breathe deeply, and I feel like this impossibly short moment has lasted longer than anything I've ever known.

"Are you okay, Miss?" I finally ask, my voice still shaky, my throat more than hoarse.

"Sydney," she says.

"What?"

"My name is not Miss; it's Sydney."

Of all the right moments for her to tell me her name, this is not one of them.

I look around us, taking out my mercifully intact high-beam flashlight and scanning the area around me. A steep, rickety staircase goes down deep into an unknown and I begin walking, Sydney following close behind.

"I already checked, there's nothing down here," she says, annoyed, as though we have any other option.

We get to the bottom and she's right. There's just

space here—empty shelves, a rug, and an emergency light that seems as though it's been on since the sixties.

"Are you sure?" I say, rifling behind the metal shelves, pressing my palms to the cemented walls. Because if there's no way out of here, then that means we're stuck here, underground with no way to get out.

My eyes flit toward the crumpled, dusty rug on the floor and I push it out of the way, dust motes flying everywhere. There on the floor is a handle, brown with rust.

Sydney gasps and pushes past me to pull on it. She pulls open the hidden door and a staircase appears, even older and more dilapidated than the one we'd just come down, leading to a place even darker and dingier than where we are now.

"We have to go, please. We have to find my brother."

She's right. We do have to go. But where can we possibly find her brother in this maze of a system, with rooms within rooms within tunnels? We'll be lucky if we make it out of here at all.

# CHAPTER 5

## Sydney

"**W**HAT? ARE YOU SERIOUSLY SCARED right now?" I say when Officer Tatum hesitates. I roll my eyes. I shouldn't be talking to a cop like this, but when you're trapped under a completely flooded subway system those kinds of social norms tend to slip.

"We have to find a way out," he says, looking at me intently. Suddenly, what he's saying make sense. He doesn't want to find Sammy, he just wants to find a way out and let some rescue team handle it.

"I told you, I'm not leaving Sammy. And isn't

that, like, what you're supposed to do? Protect and serve?" I ask.

He nods, more to himself than me, and slowly seems to resign himself. It doesn't matter whether he comes or not, I tell myself. I'll find Sammy regardless. I've been doing things for Sammy on my own for most of my life—so I prepare myself for the inevitable, but he surprises me.

"You're right," he says, and I notice that, here in the dimness, his eyes are a shocking hazel, fixed on me with a strange sort of bravery. "I'll help you find your brother."

I can't stop the shock from showing on my face. I hadn't expected him to say he'd help me. I expected him to choose himself and just try to find a way out, leaving me alone and in the dark to find Sammy. But it isn't just his kindness that surprises me. It's this other emotion that blooms inside me, one I can barely name. One that feels a lot like relief.

- - -

We get lucky—incredibly lucky—and the staircase leads to another platform and track, lit by dingy yellow emergency lights. But it's abandoned and I can't figure out what trains ever used it. We walk for what feels like hours, miles, and my mind is consumed by nervous thoughts of Sammy that make me feel absolutely crazy. So of course it's me that breaks the silence.

"Do you have any food?" I ask, because just as much as my joints ache, so does my stomach.

He swivels to look at me, his eyes narrowing in annoyance. "Food? Why would I have any food on me? I was on duty—" he says, then stops mid-sentence and reaches into his pocket. He pulls out a Clif Bar and I practically salivate at the sight. "This is all I have. Christ! I thought being trapped here was bad enough, but now we have no food. Sydney, we can't stay here and look for Sammy without food. You have to see that—" he starts, but then I remember something.

"Sammy Snacks!" I blurt out and Officer Tatum

looks at me like I'm crazy. To be honest, I feel kind of crazy. I start speaking while rifling through my messy, unorganized purse. "Sammy hates food, like he won't sit and eat a regular meal. Eating scheduled meals freaks him out for whatever reason. Too much pressure to perform or something like that. So throughout the day, I pack him lots and lots of snacks, big, small, fruit, granola bars, M&M's, juice boxes. He doesn't eat most of it, but he'll nibble at some throughout the day. He's got some with him in his backpack." He eats so little that it is definitely enough to last him a few days.

"Okay . . . Well I'm glad Sammy will have something to eat while he's stuck here."

I roll my eyes at him—again, another thing you probably shouldn't do to a cop. "I pack two, one in his backpack and one in my purse, in case I'm taking him to, like, swimming or something and he can't get to his backpack easily. Trust me, it's necessary. The kid eats like a bird. I feed him whenever I can." And finally I pull out the Ziplock bag I've been searching for. I hand it over to the officer with a satisfied grin. "Things just kind of accumulate in there." I shrug as he takes a look and marvels at the thirty-odd granola bars and smashed-up grapes.

He wrinkles his nose. "You carry around a bag of rotting fruit and granola bars?"

"Oh come on, it's mostly granola bars. You can barely smell the grapes." And the cherries, the banana, and melted Hershey's kisses.

He reaches in tentatively and grabs a granola bar, then breaks it in half. He hands me the other half and we eat in silence, our feet trudging a path along grey concrete.

But after a while, it's him that breaks the silence. "You care a lot about your brother, don't you? The snacks, the risking your life to find him . . . that's good of you."

I shrug. "If I don't, who will?"

"Your parents? Aunts or uncles if you don't have that."

"And let me guess, social services if I don't even have that."

"I'm not trying to be some nosy cop, I just don't get why you're the one who's doing all this. It just doesn't seem easy."

"And it's not," I snap, turning back to look at him. "But I'm not gonna complain about it—I'm his big sister. If there's one person who should stay tough for him, it's me."

■ ■ ■

We grow silent and the heat of the underground presses through me. I feel like I might fall, like I might slip away into my thoughts and worries. Because I'm all Sammy has and he's all I have and if I lose him because of some idiot mistake, I don't think I'll ever be the same again.

"Sydney," the cop starts. "I didn't mean to upset you. I'm—" Before he can finish, I hear the sound of electricity crackling and static moving through the air. I turn to find the direction it's coming from when Officer Tatum shouts, "Look out!" I barely have time to register, barely find time to move as I look up at one of the light fixtures and find it humming and crackling, electric sparks flying out of it. I don't even have time to scream as it tumbles toward me. Just as I expect it to hit, strong arms wrap around my torso and pull me out of the way.

Officer Tatum looks down at me, his eyes searching my face for any damage or distress, his arms still around me. I'm hardly breathing—I hear the sizzling light fixture roll on the concrete by our feet. The officer lets go and looks toward the ceiling as water begins to pour around us and more and more light fixtures begin to fall from the ceiling. It feels like the world is ending and I'm trapped in the one place where there's no chance for survival.

"The storm," I say at last, as water drips onto my face and shoulders, coating me like slick rain. "It's just as bad as they said it would be." When it let up this afternoon, we'd all assumed it was a joke. That the rain wouldn't come, that the lightning wouldn't strike, that the wind would bend to the will of us resilient New Yorkers. Officer Tatum seems to be thinking what I'm thinking, that this is more than we imagined, that finding Sammy, getting out of here, surviving this storm, won't be easy.

"No," he says after a moment. "It's worse."

# CHAPTER 6

## *Will*

**I** DON'T REALIZE HOW AFRAID I AM UNTIL THE last remaining lights began to flicker. I feel like we're on borrowed time, as though any minute they could all go out and we'd be left here. I mean, how long can we survive under here? A day—maybe two? With just granola bars and this thin, humid air. Where will we sleep? What will we do for more food?

We won't find Sammy. I've known that since the moment I chased her down these tracks. I knew that even as I told her that I would help find him. I lied to her. I looked her right in the eye and lied. Because what we needed was to find an exit, and lying was the only way to save her.

"A right turn!" she exclaims. "Sammy always makes right turns."

We turn right, just as the tunnel splits. Sydney's ability to know where her brother has headed is either uncanny or complete nonsense. Still, I can't help but feel sad for her. I don't have a brother or sister, so the only person I can imagine being in this much of a panic for is my mom, and it's not like she'd ever get lost in a subway system. Still, what's up with this kid? Why is he running off and hiding in dark, underground tunnels? When I was his age, I didn't even let go of my mom's hand at the grocery store. More than that, what did Sydney mean when she said that she was all he had? Why does it seem like he's all she has, too? Why is she the only one responsible for this little boy who seems to be more trouble than most adults could even handle?

Everything about this girl is troubling and enigmatic, from the dogged way she moves through these tunnels to the way she seems to be tougher than anyone could bargain for.

Either way, I have no choice but to follow her . . . for now, at least.

We climb a set of stairs hidden on the right-hand side of the tunnels and I release a breath of air as we continue to walk and are not greeted by another surge of water.

I check my watch as we continue walking—it's three a.m. We've been walking since about seven in the evening. About eight hours.

"Sydney," I ask. "Do you really think your brother could have gone all this way? This deep underground?" My voice is soft, tentative.

"You don't know Sammy. When he wants to stay hidden, he stays hidden. This isn't the first time he's done this," she says, and I raise an eyebrow in bewilderment.

"Not in the subway, stupid. But he's run away before. I took him to Coney Island once and he had a meltdown and hid under a concession table."

"We've been here for hours. Some of the things we've gone through to get here, could Sammy have done it all by himself?"

She doesn't say anything and I wonder if she's heard, so I continue. "What if he went another way, what if someone already found him and he's safe above ground somewhere?"

"Sammy's not like that, he wouldn't go off with a stranger. He'd probably run away and hide if someone that wasn't me tried to help him. That's why I have to be the one. That's why I have to find him."

"Even if you kill yourself in the process?" She doesn't answer and I sigh. I'm trying my hardest not to scare her away. "So what if we find a door that leads to some manhole in Times Square? Will you just go back down and keep looking?"

She's shaking, her teeth chattering, her tiny shoulders moving up and down. I put my navy blue jacket over her shoulder and she shrugs it off.

"No one told you to come chasing after me, you know. Like who told you to follow some crazy girl into the subway, anyway? Don't you have, like, a family or something? Some wife who needs you to buy spare batteries or board up some windows?"

Through the flickering lights, the trickling water, and the impending darkness, I do the one thing that I can. I let out a laugh so loud it bounces off the walls of the narrow tunnels and echoes back to us.

"A wife?" I say, the word coming out with another torrent of chuckles. "What, you think I'm married?"

"What?" she says, annoyed. "Isn't that a normal thing for men your age to do?"

"Sydney," I say, my mouth hitching in a smile that's impossible to shake. "Just how old do you think I am?" She pauses and suddenly looks unsure, her face twists into a slight scowl at being wrong.

I respond for her. "I'm nineteen."

"*Nineteen?*" she exclaims. "You're nineteen? How? You're a cop."

I laugh again, the surprise on her face is like a kid's—so unassuming and completely earnest. "I'm the youngest person in my class to graduate—young-est kid in my precinct."

"And all of New York, too, I bet."

I shrug and she glares at me before shoving me hard in the shoulder.

"You're only two years older than me, and you've been telling me what to do? What do you know?"

"I *am* an adult, technically. And can still get you in trouble for assaulting a police officer if you shove me again."

"Well, I'm not going to call you Officer Tatum anymore." She puts her hands on her hips and I snicker.

"Fine. Officer Tatum makes me sound like I have a wife, kids, and a mortgage." She shoves me again. "What is that, your fourth time assaulting a police officer? Should I round that out to a couple years in jail and community service?"

"Don't be a butt. Why are you such a young cop, anyway? Decided that college wasn't for you or something?"

It takes me a moment to find the voice to answer. And when I speak I find the laughter in my voice completely gone. "My dad was a cop. It was the only thing that made sense to me."

"Was?" she questions, probing, her eyebrows raised. I take such a sharp breath that she seems to immediately understand. "Sorry," she says, "I didn't mean to pry or whatever."

We walk in the silence of the flickering lights, water beating down on our backs, the track curving toward somewhere unknown. We pass platforms and stations long since abandoned—even before the storm, with trash heaps of sawdust, empty cardboard boxes, and candy wrappers piled around corners. Cans of empty beans stand stacked, almost as if someone had sat here to drink them all. Though that's not what startles me. What startles me are staircases that are much too dilapidated and boarded up to lead to the surface.

More hope, dashed away.

"He didn't die," I say, so long after the proposed

topic that my voice seems out of place—distant. Sydney doesn't say anything, she just waits and listens. "My dad was a cop, that's true. He didn't retire, either. He was shot. Right in the leg. He didn't do any therapy or anything, he just quit the force that same day he was released from the hospital, came home, and sat on the couch. He's been there ever since." I feel hollowed, naked, and empty. The words had left my lips without a sense of direction, and from there they'd just kept going. I have to bite my lip to keep from saying any more—about his drinking, his yelling, the awful, startling truth about everything, including myself.

I hadn't meant to say this much. I hadn't even meant to speak, but the words rose out of me the way the rain had seemed to fall from the sky this evening—expected, but still somehow surprising. I suddenly feel uncomfortable, my legs feel too long, my arms uneven, my heart irregular, this uniform much, *much* too big. I look to Sydney to see if I've made her just as awkward and unbalanced. She's looking right at me, with eyes a mix of chocolate and honey ablaze with understanding and the need to say something that I can't quite decipher.

She parts her lips as if to speak and I find my heart swelling, completely and utterly out of my control. I find I'm looking forward to what she has to say, whether in agreement or in simple acknowledgment of everything I said but shouldn't have. Someone to finally get what it is that's on my mind.

"Will," she says, her voice a low whisper. I move closer to her. "We should find a way to get some sleep. It'll be morning soon."

I deflate, but I don't let her see. I don't show my hand, I don't give away my weaknesses. I don't even clear my throat in awkwardness. I turn my face into the hard mask I learned from the academy and nod briskly.

■ ■ ■

We don't speak as we make a bed of cardboard and

rain jackets against the hard, wet floor of one of the platforms. Beneath the flickering yellow emergency lights, I curl my hands beneath my head to sleep, facing away from Sydney. I'm exhausted. I've been up for almost twenty-four hours, but sleep doesn't seem to come.

I want to say something to her—the citizen I accosted, the young woman I reprimanded, the girl I've been walking alongside for ten hours—but I still feel uneven, uncomfortable in my skin. She breaks the silence.

"My dad's not dead either," I hear her whisper from behind me, so soft it hardly seems real. "It feels like he is though." She bellows out a deep sigh that shakes the space between us. "Sometimes I feel like he left me just like this station."

"What? Abandoned?" I still don't turn to face her.

"No. Under construction."

I try to take in what that means, both for her and the space around us. Everything starts to make sense. "Under construction? What do you mean?" I ask.

She doesn't answer and I can tell she won't say more, so I change the subject.

"We must be under Second Avenue. This line has been under construction for as long as I can remember."

"Yeah, so?" she asks.

"That means somewhere, at some point, there's some sort of exit, whether it's a manhole or a construction ladder. There's a way out." I explain, but again she stays silent, our conversation from earlier seeming to echo back to us.

Because what this means for Sydney is that we won't find her brother. I'll drag her out if it means saving her life—it's my duty, to her and to my badge. It means that her heart her father left broken won't heal the way it's supposed to. That the one person who is everything to her could be lost forever to this dark, empty tunnel.

"Will!" she shouts beside me and I finally turn toward her. She's leaning up on her elbows, her eyes staring into the distance.

"Look!" she says. "Not at me, over there!" She points toward the right side of the platform, at the tracks. She jumps over me and runs toward the bumpy yellow edge of the platform. There are three different tracks on the right side, and it's impossible to tell what she's talking about, but then I see it, a flicker of something. Something flashy and purple.

Sydney jumps off the platform and races ahead. I follow, sprinting toward the flash of material, thinking that it might be our key to salvation.

"Hey!" Sydney screams as she trips over a rail, almost landing flat on her face before I catch her.

In my arms, she's a panting, breathless thing, her eyes wide with excitement and fear.

"That was *his* purple jacket. That was Sammy. My Sammy!" she says.

# CHAPTER 7

## *Sydney*

"**I**'M TELLING YOU, THAT WAS HIM. I KNOW what I saw," I tell Officer . . . Will. I tell Will. God, I'm on a first-name basis with a cop. What the hell is this subway doing to me? Well, according to Will, it's making me crazy.

"I'm not saying you don't."

"You just don't believe me."

"Hey, I saw something, too, but that could have easily been a scrap of something blowing in the wind."

I laugh. "What? You feel a breeze somewhere? In the middle of the frigging underground?" Will rolls his eyes, something that I've learned is his signature move. He's like a kid in grown-up clothes—or the other way around. Or maybe just both. Always rolling his eyes or crossing his arms or not believing you when you tell him you saw your baby brother and not a ghost. Though I do have to admit, it is fun messing with him.

"Well, there's nothing here," he says. It might be fun messing with Will, but it's not at all fun admitting when he's right. And he might be. After we saw that flash of color, we ran to where we thought we saw it—the third track, but that track wasn't even completed yet. It ended in a pile of iron and metal. No Sammy, no purple rain jacket in sight.

"So what, we're just going to give up?"

"No. We need to get some sleep. It's five in the morning. You can't tell me you aren't exhausted." I'm not. At least I don't feel it. There's too much desperate energy inside me, a coil of nerves and feeling. But Will looks more than exhausted. He looks like a zombie. His hazel eyes are rimmed red and his pale peachy skin is taut and sallow. I wonder how I look. My dark skin usually doesn't show any signs of fatigue, but I imagine that with all the humidity and rain, my hair's a giant ball of hot mess. The more I think about it, I have been feeling kind of out of it lately. Maybe I am wrong—maybe I hadn't seen Sammy. Maybe I'd missed some hidden right turn and I'm completely in the wrong direction. Maybe Sammy's been found by some rescue team we hadn't encountered and he's warm under a blanket on the surface.

Maybe things are not as bad as they seem—at least that is what I try telling myself.

"Come on, Syd. Let's try to sleep," he says, and at the sound of "Syd," I straighten up. No one calls me Syd—not ever. The only person who did left me and never looked back. I open my mouth to correct him—to yell or scream or tell him to back off—but it's strangely nice. The way "Syd" rumbles in his throat in a way that's both soothing and disquieting.

And it's more than that. I feel guilty. He did all this for me—risked his life to help me find Sammy.

I do as the officer says and lie down atop the cardboard, but this time we face each other.

He closes his eyes first and we fall asleep to the sound of dropping rain, flickering lights, and the steady hum of our breathing.

- - -

I wake up to shaking, the concrete floor humming beneath me, the light fixtures swaying to and fro. This has been happening for a while now—violent tremors shaking the entire underground due to the violence of Hurricane Angelica. I don't even want to think about what's going on up there. I don't even want to think about my mother or Ezra or Kathy. It's too much—especially when my mind is so focused on Sammy.

I check my phone, which is miraculously still charged, and see that it's ten a.m., but time doesn't seem to matter here. How can it, when the only thing here is darkness and water?

Of course Will is already up, squeezing excess water out of his dark blue shirt, his hair already perfectly smoothed back, looking tailored in sleek military precision. He's sitting on a flattened cardboard box a few feet from his makeshift bed. He stops squeezing the water out of his jacket and places it beside himself so he can study something in his hands. Turning it over and over again between his fingers.

"What's that?" I ask and he startles at my voice, hazel eyes flickering up to meet mine. For a moment, he doesn't look like a cop. Not in his white T-shirt, not with his dirty boots and tired eyes. He looks his age, young and strangely cute.

My cheeks redden at the thought. God, I need to get a grip.

"It's a baseball," he says, handing me the small white ball. I turn it over in my fingers, studying the bumpy red stitches.

"A baseball? Do you think it belonged to one of the workers down here?"

Will shakes his head. "Why would they bring a baseball down here? This isn't the kind of place you play a game of catch in."

"What are you getting at?"

Will looks at me for a moment before scratching his head. "I don't know. I just wonder who could have left it here. This isn't an active station. Who's been here before?"

I let out a loud laugh, and just as I expect, he rolls his eyes. "Now who's the one being crazy?"

He snorts. "Still you, I'm just speculating. You were ready to chase a ghost through a mountain of metal."

I laugh back at him, and the pressure that has been inside my chest since we've been down here eases a bit. We smile at each other, ridiculous and grinning, trapped in this maze of tunnel. God, I can't believe I'd ever thought he had a wife and kids. It's so obvious now, everything about him, from the dimple in his cheek to the way his eyes crinkle when he smiles, just screams young. Too young.

We start our morning by walking, splitting granola bars and raisins between the two of us. We talk comfortably, as though something about last night—everything about last night—made us friends somehow.

"Pass me the ball," I say with a smile, referencing the ratty baseball he's been passing between his hands.

"You play?" he asks as we continue walking. He surprises me by throwing it fast to the side, but my reflexes are faster and I catch it before it falls into a puddle on the ground.

"When I was a kid—not so much now. I still love baseball, though. Ezra and I were supposed to go to a Mets game in the fall, but, well, that's not gonna happen." Especially since we're trapped down here. Especially since we're broken up.

The mere mention of this name is enough to get me upset and wound up.

"Who's Ezra?" Will inquires as we walk, and I pass the ball back to him, trying my best not to make a face. I'm not in the mood to talk about Ezra anymore. I wish I'd never even brought it up.

"Just some guy," I say, and I see Will raise an eyebrow beside me.

Instead, we talk about our friends, school, and the police academy, passing the ball between us as we move along.

We talk about what it's like to have a father and yet feel fatherless without going into too much detail. We say nothing about circumstance—only feelings. The crushing weight of your own disappointment, the constant quest for approval, the bumpy, jagged scars on your heart that never seem to really go away.

"So he left you. Is that why you're the one who's got to look out for Sammy?"

"No. I mean, yes. That's partly it. I mean, my mom is a nurse and she has to take double shifts to keep up with our rent." I say, repeating the exact line she's always given me, my voice numb and not interested at all in talking more about her. Though, it always feels like a lie. I always wonder if she works more on purpose just so she can avoid us. Just because she's not sure if she can handle being a mother to Sammy. "But Sammy, he . . . he's got some issues."

Will nods as though he knew all along. Because what kind of kid would go running through the subway system? What other kid wouldn't make a noise about losing the only adult with them? Still, I'm angry. I don't want him assuming anything about my brother.

"Well, they're not issues, exactly," I say, and Will just nods again. "It's just the way he is. The way he's built. It's almost like a personality trait." *Almost*, I say to myself. *Just almost.*

"I knew a girl with Asperger's. At the academy. She'd walk through the halls taking every left turn whenever she felt agitated."

I stop and swivel to look at him, my anger rising

for a reason I can't exactly pinpoint. "Don't tell me some fake academy story thinking you can relate to me. Sammy's my brother. No one else knows what it's like. You don't know what it's like." I don't want to yell at him like this, but I can't help it. I can't help but feel destructive and angry. I wish Sammy was here. Oh God, all I want is to find him. To hold him in my arms and give him the kind of hug that only I'm allowed to give him.

I storm away from Will, yelling that I'm off to pee so he doesn't follow me. I find a quiet corner and take a deep breath, trying to soothe my nerves and thanking God my diet's so fiber-poor that I don't need to go number two yet.

I try to hold myself together, even as the lights flutter around me. Even as a steady stream of water flows down my neck. I stay tough, not for my dad, not for me, but for Sammy. I gotta stay tough for Sammy.

As if someone out there has read my thoughts, I

see it again. That flash of purple material running across the tracks.

"Sammy?" I whisper in disbelief, my heart hammering. This time it's no longer a flash: a figure pops out from behind a rail post and begins to run. Not just a figure. A boy. A boy in a purple raincoat.

# CHAPTER 8

## *Will*

I HEAR SYDNEY SCREAM AND I RUN AS FAST AS I can, my breath hitching in my throat as I assume the worst. It's not because she's seen a rat or something. We've seen about thirty of those down here and not once have I seen that girl flinch. She reminds me of Captain Gerri in the way that she doesn't seem to be afraid of anything. But something, or maybe someone, has made her scream.

I think back to the baseball. Back to the sneaking suspicion I had of someone else being down here with us. Sydney had called me crazy and maybe I was—but I couldn't help it. I couldn't stop my mind from wandering from place to place. And now she is screaming and that was the only thought that went through my mind. Finally I see her and she's running. And I'm right—and yet I'm so very wrong.

There is someone else down here. Someone in a purple rain jacket.

"Sammy!" Sydney screams again. She found him. She found her little brother. The one I'd so callously tried to pretend that I understood. *Stupid. Stupid. Stupid.* No wonder she ran away from me—I was an idiot.

But now Sammy was here and the only thing we had to worry about was finding a way home.

"Sammy!" I scream with her and run faster, finally catching up to her. Together we run toward the little boy in the purple raincoat, our breaths coming out hard and fast and in unison.

The boy keeps running though, and even I can see the confusion on her face. This must not be like him. He wouldn't have come when a stranger like me called him but he's used to her. He knows her.

He should come when she calls. Yet he's not stopping, he's moving almost faster, taking the curves of the tunnels like he's done it a hundred times before.

"Sammy?" Sydney questions and I hear her voice break. The last thing I want is to see her cry, I realize, this brave girl who carried her brother and all his complexities on her thin shoulders. So I run even faster, faster than I think I've run in my entire life, and hook my arm around the boy's shoulders. The boy and I tumble to the ground. Sydney catches up with me and helps me and the boy up. Together we stare down at a boy with brown hair, large, dark eyes, and rich, tawny skin.

"That's not him. That's not Sammy," she says, and the boy looks up at her in fear and awe. But on the left breast of his jacket in small black lettering is the name "Sammy."

"That's his jacket," she says, the tears spilling down her cheeks, and there's nothing I can do to stop it.

I turn to the boy in Sammy's jacket and glower at

him. My police officer mask is affixing itself onto my face, turning me stern and serious.

"Who are you? What are you doing here? Why do you have this jacket? What happened to the boy who was wearing it?"

Sydney doesn't say a word; the tears falling down her face silently, her eyes blank.

The young boy looks between the two of us, his eyes wide and scared.

"I-I-I'm Jaime," he says after a moment. "This is my jacket."

"Listen, kid. I'm a cop, you don't want to lie to me," I say, trying my best to sound intimidating yet kind at the same time. I mean he's just a kid. He's what, maybe nine years old? What's he doing down here in the middle of a storm in a place as hard to get to as this? Where are his parents?

"Don't lie," I repeat. "You don't want to find out what happens if you do," I say, and the kid looks so scared I almost feel guilty, but Sydney needs to find Sammy. I'm afraid of what will happen if she doesn't.

"I found it," he says. "On the ghost tracks."

"The what?"

"The Fifty-Seventh Street stop," the little boy—Jaime—says.

This time, Sydney cuts in. "You're lying. We were just there. It's completely submerged under water." We'd barely escaped with our lives.

"Not that one. That's the one everyone uses. I'm talking about the one no one knows about. The ghost tracks."

There was that term again. The ghost tracks—as if there were such thing.

"And what were you doing down by these ghost tracks? What are you doing here?"

Jaime shrugs. "I live here."

I want to laugh at the impossibility of it all. It's absolutely ridiculous. Yet there's something about the earnest way he talks that tells me he's serious.

That he actually believes he lives underground here in the subway.

I pull out the baseball from my pocket and show it to him. "And this—is this yours?" Before I can even think to ask him any more questions, he grabs it from my hands with a bright, childlike eagerness. He smiles, his fingers turning the ball over in his hand toward an exact location. Under the red stitching is his name etched out in blue ink, "Jaime." I'd missed that. I'd missed that completely. I was trained to catch details like this. Grueling months at the academy taught me better than that, and yet I'd still missed it.

It must have been Sydney—her sneaking up on me this morning, completely disarming me with her caustic smile and ready laugh. The strange mention of that random guy Ezra, who was supposed to take her out to a Mets game. "Just some guy" who was probably, maybe, her boyfriend. I shake the thought of them together, and the strange emotion it provokes, out of my head. This girl is going to drive me insane.

"Hey, kiddo," Sydney leans down next to the kid, her tears no longer flowing but still wet on her cheeks. "My friend Will and I have been looking everywhere for the boy who owns this jacket. His name is Sammy. Purple is his favorite color."

"Mine, too!" The boy gives Sydney a soft smile and she beams back at him, radiant. She's great at talking to kids. I, on the other hand, apparently suck at it.

"You should help us find him. You could be part of our team. It could be like an adventure. Then afterward, we can get you back to your mom and dad." She smiles again, and it's the brightest thing in this tunnel.

"Mom and Dad?" Jaime asks, tilting his head upward in confusion.

"Yeah," I say. "Aren't you lost? Don't you want to find them?"

Jaime lets out a snicker. "I'm not lost. I told you,

I live here. With both of them—my mom and my dad."

Sydney and I share a look. This little kid is obviously not all together, but we don't let our confusion show. This time we both smile at him, and I try to look as welcoming as possible.

"So what do you say, Jaime? Do you want to help find Sammy? My little brother?"

"Sure, but first I think I should take you to see my parents. They're the ones who could probably help. I don't know much about the ghost tracks."

His parents? Ghost tracks? How long has this kid been trapped down here?

Before we can question him, a violent tremor rocks us backward and Sydney stumbles into me. I keep her steady and place her back on her feet. Jaime looks back and forth between the two of us.

"What's going on up there?" he asks. His dark eyes question us, his eyebrow raised and his face a mask of confusion.

"What do you mean, hon?" asks Sydney.

"There's been a lot of shaking and the lights keep going off. There's water, too. So much water. It's everywhere."

He doesn't know. How it is possible that this kid doesn't know about the biggest hurricane to hit New York in more than a century? Sydney and I share another look before she leans down to talk to Jaime.

"Don't worry about what's up there. As long as you're here with us, nothing can hurt you. My friend Will here is a cop and he's basically my own personal bodyguard. So if you come with us and help us find Sammy, he can protect you too."

Protect. The one thing I'd sworn to do since I finished the academy. Even before then. But could I? Yesterday was my first day on the job and I'd barely managed to protect Sydney.

Jaime considers this. His big eyes seem to take in everything about us, from our clothes to our hair and the tiredness on our faces. Eventually he gestures for us to follow him.

"Come on," he says. "There's a lot to show you."

We follow him as he scurries ahead, just slightly out of earshot, giving us time to speak without him listening.

"What are we doing?"

"Is it not obvious?" Sydney responds, a smile bright on her lips. "Following some strange kid on some subway tracks to find another strange kid."

I roll my eyes. "Let's be serious," I say, even though part of me wants to indulge in her giddiness and laugh too. How happy she must be, to be this close to finding her brother. Still, this is too strange. Something is not right.

"But why is he here? How can we trust him?" I ask.

"I don't know, Will. But this is the only chance we have. Plus, aren't you worried about this kid? I mean, he thinks he lives down here in the subway. You're a cop. Isn't it, like, your job to do something about this? Protect him?"

There's that word again—protect. It's like a hot

knife to my stomach. I wince and Sydney raises an eyebrow, worry seeming to cloud her features.

"Will?" she asks. "Are you okay?"

I don't know what to tell her. I'm not okay. I'm trapped here underground in this uniform and I feel powerless. Being down here makes me feel like I've failed to do the one thing I swore to do. A feeling that's not at all unfamiliar.

"Will," she says again as we continue to follow Jaime. "You know, you never finished telling me why you became a cop."

I didn't? I thought I had, but as I think back on it, I hadn't. Just part of the story.

"I became an officer because of my dad," I reiterate, not sure if I can let myself tell her as much as I did last time, or even the rest of it. But Sydney's more intuitive than I've given her credit for.

"I know that's not all. Your dad getting shot, it's not the only reason why you're a cop. If it was, when you spoke about him there'd be a sense of respect in your voice. Pride that you were following in his foot-steps. Not this . . . " She searches for a word.

"What? Not this what?" I dare her to say something. *Anything.*

Her honey-colored eyes meet mine, fierce and unyielding.

"Anguish," she finishes and I release a breath I hadn't realized I'd been holding. I should feel exposed, uncomfortable . . . afraid, even. Instead, quiet relief begins to fill my chest and I find myself moving my lips to speak.

"My dad, after he got shot, he wasn't just lazy and not there, he was scary. He wouldn't hit my mom, he wouldn't hit us. But there was something in his eyes—this glint. As if any minute he could have done it. Any minute he could have let his self-loathing and anger take over and hurt us. He'd break chairs around the house, press cigarette butts into the walls, throw things around his room, almost as if he was getting ready to strike. And that's why I became a cop, so if he ever did try anything, I'd be ready. So I'd be strong enough to handle it."

I don't know why I'm telling her all this—we just met. There's just something about the darkness of this tunnel and the steadiness of her eyes that makes this feel natural. Safe.

I see her shake her head, her dark hair glittering in the dim light of the few emergency lamps above us. "You don't need that uniform to make you strong, Will. You don't."

I breathe out.

I want to say something back to her—a refusal, a denial, or maybe even an expression of gratitude—but Jaime runs back to us, taking Sydney's hand in his own, pulling her along.

"Come on, let's hurry. We'll be there soon."

# CHAPTER 9

*Sydney*

DON'T REALIZE HOW SCARED I AM UNTIL I hold Jaime's hand. Until I feel how small it is between my fingers. So much like Sammy's, except not. Not chubby in the way his are, not fidgety and a little shaky. Not mine.

I swallow my fear and follow Jaime into the darkness with Will close behind, a truckload of confessions in the air between us. Jaime takes us through a path I wouldn't even have noticed otherwise. It's a small archway under construction beyond the tracks. He takes us through and I wonder how I'm ever going to find Sammy—how I'll ever even get home.

The mystery of this boy—Jaime—is somehow the answer to all our problems. He has Sammy's jacket and he seems to know his way around the subway a great deal more than anyone ought to.

And what's craziest of all is he hasn't been outside in days—maybe weeks or months. After all, how could he not know about the storm? How could this be news to him? Where has he been hiding all this time?

"It's just a little farther," says Jaime in that little kid voice of his that reminds me so much of Sam's—even though Sammy was never the type of kid people thought of as conventionally adorable.

"You're going to love my family," says Jaime, and Will and I share a look. He's been saying stuff like this since the moment I took his hand and he began leading us closer.

I can't do anything but give a soft smile. It's just too hard to imagine what this kid must have gone through to make him believe that his family lives in the subway.

"How do you know where to find them?" asks Will from behind me. I steal a glance at him and catch the look of distrust on his face. He eyes Jaime's hand in mine as if willing me to step away, but this boy is so young—what's there to mistrust? If anything, we should be helping him.

Jaime shrugs in response to Will's question but the officer persists.

"How do you know your way around here?"

"Because I live here, duh."

"For how long?"

"Always."

Jaime begins humming a bright tune, swinging our joined hands between us. The sound of his song echoes through the vast tunnels and sends a chill down my spine.

"Are you not scared?" I ask softly. "Living down here in the dark?"

I think of Sammy, huddled in some corner somewhere, humid air and darkness pressing in on him, the sounds of leaks and falling rain too much for him to bear.

"No," says Jaime. "What's there to be afraid of?"

And he's right I guess. The worst that can happen is a rat deciding to crawl on your foot while you're sleeping. There's no noise down here, no violence, no crime, no storm. In some ways, being stuck down here is much safer than being on the surface and out in the open.

It almost feels like we're hiding down here—away from the rest of the world.

"We're here," says Jaime suddenly, after we make an abrupt right turn.

I push myself out of my thoughts and look at the space around us. There are no tracks here, just heaps of metal and tools. The space is also wider and taller than any other section we've been in. Almost as if someone started to create a tunnel down here, then just got too lazy to finish.

But it's entirely devoid of people—it's entirely devoid of Sammy.

Will grabs the boy away from me. "Where's Sammy? You said he'd be here," he says sternly in the kind of voice that commands authority. I steal a quick glance at his face. Suddenly, everything he's told me about his dad fits into this persona he puts on. Will—the cop. I can see just how much it's shaped him.

He's not the only one with a messed-up father. For not the first time, I start to wonder just how much my father's absence has shaped me. I mean, I doubt I'd be some spoiled princess if he was still around. Still, what would change? What would be different?

I push my thoughts away again and quickly step in, putting a gentle hand on Jaime's shoulder. "No. He didn't. He said he'd take us to his parents." And then find Sammy? Hopefully, possibly, maybe?

Jaime shrinks toward me, but continues to walk toward the middle of the empty space.

"I'm home!" he screams, but, just as I thought, no one answers him. He yells again that he's home, and Will and I watch as he's met again by silence. If I'm honest with myself, I hadn't really expected any different. This boy has obviously been here for a long time—so long that he's lost any sense of reality.

I give Will a look as Jaime keeps yelling in the dark. "This feels like a scene in a slasher film, just before the main characters get offed by some lady with a chainsaw. You know, when the theater gets all quiet 'cause something bad's about to happen."

Will shrugs, his eyes keenly focused on the room around him, disregarding my joke and surveying the scene around us like a cop. "I don't really get around to going to the theaters, let alone for horror movies."

"What?" I try a laugh again, just to lighten the mood. "Even Ezra watches horror films, and the guy's afraid of everything." Especially things like leaving his house without properly moisturizing or ripping one of his leather pants. Well, at least the pants fear is legitimate, they really are obscenely tight.

Will turns to look at me, eyes narrowed. "Well, not all of us have time to date."

Shock widens my eyes and I open my mouth to protest when a loud clamoring fills the space.

"Jaime, how many times do I have to tell you to watch how loud you are? What if father was napping? Come, you must be hungry. I made break—" A woman looks at us in shock, seemingly coming from out of the shadows. Will and I both take a step back, and I look at her hands to see what's in them. Thankfully, it's not a chainsaw.

"Jaime," she starts in a hushed, almost afraid, tone. "Who are these people?"

"They're my new friends," Jaime says. The woman continues to scrutinize us and I'm beyond confused—beyond freaked out. She's has long, tight curls pushed out of her face and a rag in her hand as if she's just finished washing the dishes—as if beyond the shadows of this cavern is some kind of loving, white-picket-fence home.

Will speaks first, his voice coming out confident and sure, but his words are anything but.

"This—you're his mother."

The woman comes closer, putting the rag casually on her shoulder and reaching for Jaime, placing him firmly behind her back. Her eyes track us coolly in the dimness—cold and insect-like. It's almost as if she's dissecting us. I don't know why, but it makes me uneasy and I try to stop myself from squirming under her gaze.

"You live down here?" Will asks, and I'm too shocked to even chime in.

The woman nods.

"In the subway," Will says again, sounding a little more than dumbfounded.

"And you obviously live up there. So what are you doing all the way out here? How did you meet my son?" She raises her eyebrows, those calculating eyes assessing us like we're under a petri dish. She's dressed in tall brown boots, kept together with duct tape, and a large men's sweater, riddled with holes, falling down to her knees. Everything about her looks different and alien from us. I'm still in my date clothes from earlier—jeans and a cute top—and Will's dressed like a police officer.

I interject and tell her the story as solemnly as I can, about Sammy, his running away, meeting Will—how we've been looking for Sammy since yesterday afternoon, about Jaime and his purple jacket. Will shoots me a look when I finish, as though I shouldn't have given so much away—especially to this woman who's stranger than anyone I've ever met.

But what can I do? We can't expect her to explain her situation if we don't explain ours.

"Forgive me," she smiles, a stiff, almost pained smile. "We live off the clothes and items we scavenge. Jaime surely wouldn't have taken the clothes of someone he knew still needed them."

Scavenge? In the subway? Who are these people?

"I'm sorry," Will says. "I still don't understand. You can't live down here." I hear the edge in his voice, the need to add "it's illegal" to what he's just said. He doesn't even have to—you can see it in his stance, in the way he holds himself high above the woman and her son—even me. The honorable, the strict, the precise Officer Will is back and it feels as though he's never left. Somehow that thought makes me want to step away from him.

"Surely you've heard of people like me before, officer." She says "officer" with obvious distaste in her voice, no longer trying to hide her distrust under a fake smile.

Suddenly, what she's saying strikes a chord and I raise my chin to look her in the eye. "Mole people. You're a mole person!" I exclaim in disbelief. It doesn't even sound real—but that's what she is. I remember watching a documentary about them in the ninth grade, baby Sammy sitting alongside me in rapt attention. He'd been so curious—asking questions about these homeless people that decided that the underground was a safer place to live than the metropolis of New York. But there aren't people like that anymore—the city has fixed up home-less shelters, created more job programs. There is no actual need to live down here—not one that is practical and makes sense. I remember going to bed that night, confident that this was a problem that had been eradicated sometime in the nineties. That Sammy's interest in them was something passing and unsubstantial—that he wouldn't grow up and want to leave society like that, no matter how much he seemed to be detached from it.

"I didn't realize . . ." Will starts, "that people still did this." Apparently he'd been thinking the same thing I was.

"Of course you didn't. People on the surface never look past their own noses, let alone far enough down that they'd see people like us." She puts her hand on her hips, her voice holding a sharp, cold edge. A terse smile stays on her face. Her eyes narrow as Jaime stands still and uncertain between us.

"I'm Margo," she says finally, resigned. "And this is my camp." She picks up a lantern from the ground and lights it in one fluid motion. The space around us floods with more light than I've seen in hours. And suddenly, I see it—the shadows where she seemed to come from are not shadows at all. Far off, next to a pile of metal, rubber, and abandoned industrial tools, are three empty subway cars—old enough to be from a time my mother wasn't even born. Around these rust-covered train cars are different-colored blankets and pieces of cloth hitched on tall metal pipes or wooden sticks.

I peer inside, letting in a sharp breath when I make out what's there. People. Mole people. All ages, all sizes, all races—huddled together, peering at us with wide eyes adjusting to the lantern's light. There aren't many of them—maybe seven or eight—but it's enough that I'm more than a little intimidated. Especially if they're going to assess us the way Margo has so far.

A man comes forward out of the train car and approaches us. He's tall with a broad smile that almost can't be faked.

"Dad!" Jaime runs toward him and grabs onto his fingers. "Look at the friends I brought."

He must have heard everything we've said before, because he's not as startled as Margo was.

"Hello," he says brightly. "My name is Ruiz. And you all are?"

I look between Jaime's parents—Margo and Ruiz. Definitely not as imaginary as I thought.

"I'm Sydney Mendoza and this is Officer Will Tatum. We're looking for a little boy. Blond hair, very smart, kind of shy."

"A little boy?" Ruiz looks at Margo, his face confused. "Jaime and I were out for a walk earlier today when I thought I saw someone on the ghost tracks. When we went closer, we didn't' see anyone, just a purple raincoat. I assumed the dark was playing a trick on me and took the coat for Jaime. I didn't realize that anyone else would be this deep down here."

My heart stutters. It isn't until this moment that I realize that I've feared the worst. That part of me has assumed that something bad happened to Sammy—that he was hurt somewhere and it was all my fault. But I feel like some sort of tension in me has been released. Tears spill down my cheeks completely out of my control. I don't normally cry—especially in front of other people—but I can't help it. Sammy is out there. I let myself dare to hope, to dream, to pray that Sammy and I will make it out of here.

"Take me," I say. "You have to take me to where you found him. You have to take me to those ghost tracks."

# CHAPTER 10

*Will*

**H**ONESTLY, WHO WOULD HAVE GUESSED that the subway could be this complex? This is ridiculous. And I'm not even talking about the group of people who actually live down here.

Ruiz explains what ghost tracks are as he and Margo lead us toward them, and I think that this day can't get any weirder.

"They're abandoned subway tracks—the one we're heading to right now were started in the sixties and never finished. There's more stuff like that than you'd realize. There are tons of abandoned routes down here that just get forgotten over time. This place is bigger than most people know."

He didn't have to tell me; Sydney and I have been here for longer than anyone ought to. From now on, if I need to get somewhere, I'll take a friggin' Uber.

But Ruiz, Margo, Jaime? They'd lived here for even longer. Jaime might have lived here his entire life. It was hard to be sure with these people. Something about them seemed off, other than the fact that they lived their lives in a place most people would never consider living in.

"Have you guys always lived down here?" I ask. Sydney elbows me sharply in the ribs as if I shouldn't have asked that and I glare back at her. For a moment, I wonder if she's like this with that Ezra guy, her probable, maybe boyfriend. Always pushing and shoving and bossing around. I wonder how he can take it, especially if he's the kind of guy who's scared of everything when Sydney is so clearly afraid of almost nothing. Somehow that doesn't seem to be the type of guy she'd go for. If they are dating, that is.

I stomp this line of thought down and focus on Ruiz.

Ruiz doesn't seem to think I'm being rude at all and he replies with a laugh. "I wasn't born here if that's what you're asking. And neither was Jaime. We moved when he was young enough to not remember much of the surface."

Move. As if he packed up his house in a moving van and moved from Harlem to Brooklyn—like he's not basically living in the sewers. As though she can hear my thoughts, Sydney raises her eyebrows at me. She thinks I'm judging them too harshly. But it's hard not to—they have a child. A son that doesn't seem to know anything about the outside world. A kid who's probably never been to school.

Maybe I think this just because I'm a cop, but how can this be someone's only option? I want to say something, anything, to let them know how wrong I think this is—but I can't. Not until we find Sammy, not until they help us.

"This must be where they last saw him," says Margo. She's not as warm as Ruiz is, just cold, curt, and unnervingly polite, as if she's counting the seconds until we leave. Sydney seems just as rattled by her as I do, yet she's trusting her, something I can't quite bring myself to do. For any of these people. Ruiz seems to agree with Margo as he looks around.

"How did he look? Was he okay? Did he seem scared?" Sydney chimes in, her voice hopeful and desperate all at once. It breaks my heart. I watch as she tries to hold it all together, her shaky tone the only thing betraying her composure. I wonder, for maybe the hundredth time, what would have happened if I hadn't stopped her. If I had helped her immediately. Would she have found Sammy by now? Is this my fault somehow? Could I have been better to her? These questions filter in through my guilt and, despite myself, I take her hand in mine almost as if to lend her strength. She squeezes back and somehow I'm comforted. Somehow in her touch, she conveys just how strong she is—how fearless and brave—and it feels like everything is going to be okay.

"I'm sorry, child. As I said earlier, I didn't get a good look at him. These tunnels can get pretty dark."

"And you're okay with that?" I ask immediately, Sydney's hand in mine somehow making me feel stronger. "With living your life down here in the dark? Never seeing the sun again?"

Ruiz laughs again. "You surface people think that the light is so great. That it's the dark that's scary. But it's just the opposite." He doesn't explain more and instead continues along, as if his lifestyle is much too nuanced to bother explaining to us. I roll my eyes at his turned back just as Sydney pulls her hand out of mine and rushes to catch up to them.

As always, there's nothing I can do but follow her.

- - -

It feels like hours later when we stop our walk along the ghost tracks, Sammy still nowhere to be found.

"It seems like your brother is not on these tracks. He must have taken another path from here," Margo says in that brusque tone of hers. She turns to Sydney. "If you don't mind my asking, why did Sammy run away from you? Was he upset?"

I don't like the way she says "run away from you." As if Sydney did something to provoke him, as if this is all her fault. I hope she doesn't take the bait and blame herself. I turn and watch as Sydney's eyes turn livid and I want to smile. Of course she wouldn't let this woman get under her skin.

"Sammy has Asperger's. He doesn't act like everyone else does when there's a lot going on. He runs and hides—not from me, but from everything." You would think that that would be enough to shut Margo down, but the woman's eyes stay shrewd.

"From the world," she says softly, then begins walking ahead of us, back toward the direction of the camp, seemingly giving up on helping us find Sammy today.

Ruiz gives us an apologetic smile. "My wife can be a little critical of the surface world. I'm really sorry about that." But Margo wasn't just being critical of the surface world; she was being critical of Sydney.

"Hey!" I bark at her and Margo slows her pace but doesn't turn. "I said, hey!" This time she stops and crosses her arms, looking me squarely in the eyes.

"Yes, officer?" she says, almost mockingly.

"Do you have any idea what's going on up there? The worst storm in New York history has flooded most of this system and, if it's this bad down here, what do you think's going on up there? What do you think it was like on that subway platform for that little boy who hates being touched? It was all bodies, shoving and fighting for their lives. There was nothing Sydney could have done except what she's doing now—chase after her younger brother and do whatever it takes to find him."

I finish on a shuddering breath and Margo stares at me, her lips pressing into a thin line.

"Then I wish you both luck in getting to the surface." Cold, calm, and unsettling, her voice drops to an almost-whisper.

She looks between the two of us, her eyes narrowing almost imperceptibly before she turns on her heel. We walk back toward their camp in silence.

- - -

Sydney won't talk to me. It must be well into the evening now, more than twenty-four hours since we've been here, and I'm starving. My stomach is grumbling for something other than granola bars and raisins, and all I want is for Sydney to turn around and talk to me, but she stares straight ahead.

We sit on a medley of different chairs, buckets, and stepping stools around a small bonfire, roasting some questionable meat and heating up cans of beans. The camp isn't as bad as I thought it would be. The dwellers—mole people, as Sydney called them—are all happy and bright-faced, telling stories around the fire and laughing with one another. An older man with a graying beard plays an out-of-tune guitar and people dance against the faint lights of the fire. Even Margo smiles from time to time, stroking Jaime's head and laughing as Ruiz comes close and whispers into her ear.

They're like a family—down where the rain doesn't hit and the storm is nonexistent. Their lives are untouched, unruffled by the turmoil of the outside world. The storm is probably pretty much over by now, anyway. It's only a matter of time before rescue crews start moving through these tunnels— only a matter of when.

I try to catch Sydney's eye, but she still won't look back. With her dark hair pulled to one side, the fire illuminates the soft angle of her jaw, the brightness of her eyes. It's strange how I only met her yesterday. I feel like we've been down here for weeks—I feel like I've *known* her for weeks. And not because

I feel like we have some strange, instant cosmic connection—I'm not crazy. It's just that so much has happened since I yelled "Miss!" out into a crowd of panicked commuters. So much has happened since I vowed that I would get us out of here no matter what. I'd felt so much older than her, like I was so much more responsible. Now she's the one who seems braver, stronger. It's the way she pushed her way through these people, the way she's navigating this situation as if it's nothing. Even the way she laughs freely at the jokes people start telling around the fire is fierce and independent. She isn't afraid of any of these people. Even if she's wary of them, she'd never let any of that show.

"So are you kids planning on staying or what?" asks an old woman, who may or may not be blind. She says "kids," but she's looking more into the fire than at us.

"We're just here for her brother," I say sternly. I'm not like Sydney. I won't pretend that this situation sits well with me.

The woman lets out a hearty laugh. "Well y'all should. This place's got everything you need and more. Margo and Ruiz do a good job of keeping us happy, that's for sure. Ain't it, Jaime?"

The little boy chimes in with a cheery smile and lifts up a meat kebab in salute. I sniff at my piece of meat and decide that I'm too hungry not to take a bite.

I'm not surprised that Margo and Ruiz run this whole thing though. It makes sense—everyone looks at them with the kind of respect and awe you can't fake.

Ruiz smiles, putting his arm around his wife lovingly.

"So why did you choose to come down here?" Sydney asks, directing the question toward the couple.

"Choose?" Margo turns the friendly tone Sydney used into something aggressive. Her normally cold tone turns sharper than usual. "Who told you we had a choice? The world up there is a cancer, okay?

A cancer. And everyone there is slowly dying and they don't even know it. It's like one of those sleeper agents. The noise, the pollution, the violence, and the greed—slowly killing them one by one. And the worst part is, they're all a part of it—all willingly a part of their own deaths. I used to be a part of it, too. Until I decided that enough was enough and I couldn't deal with paying that society every month in taxes and mortgages. Until I decided that I needed to live in peace. That's why we came here. So we could live and breathe in peace."

We stare at her in shock. Peace. Under a dirty subway system. Where there's no running water, no grocery stores? Margo merely sits back down, her cool eyes holding a glint in them I can't quite interpret. And looking at her, it almost makes sense. In a way this place is kind of peaceful. It's calming and weirdly relaxing being so far away from responsibilities and the drama of the real world.

I look at Sydney and see her brows furrowed, and I wonder if she's contemplating the same thing.

We eat in front of the fire and don't speak much for the rest of the evening. Still, Sydney won't look at me—she won't speak to me.

Eventually I can't take it and tap her on the shoulder when we finish eating, the rest of the camp too preoccupied with their conversations to take notice.

"Hey, you okay?"

What I really want to say is this: *Are we okay? Are you mad at me? Did I do something to break the small bit of friendship between us?*

"I'm fine," she says and gets up to walk a little ways away. I stand, too, and softly touch her elbow.

"Syd."

She freezes at the sound of her nickname.

"Don't call me that."

"I'm sorry. I didn't mean t—"

She suddenly whirls around to glare at me.

"Good. You should be. We don't know each other. You can't go around calling me cute nicknames like Syd."

I stare back at her, shocked, reaching for something to say—but she's right. I can't call her that. We've only known each other for a day. Yet she can't deny that after everything, after all we've been through, that there's a strand of something between us. Something tenuous and fragile—something like friendship.

But maybe I've crossed a line in my feelings or my actions, I can't tell. Maybe the paranoia I've had about that Ezra kid has been right all along. Maybe he is her boyfriend. Maybe she loves him and has no room in her life for surprising possible friendships with cops.

"Sorry, I know that you're with someone. I shouldn't have—"

The fury in her eyes grows and is unmistakable now.

"What? With someone? You think just because I don't want you to call me Syd, it means that I already have a boyfriend? Are you joking?" She looks about ready to saw my head off.

"No . . . wait . . . I wasn't being . . . that's not it. That's not what I meant. No . . . I . . . " The words are not coming out elegantly at all. I want to shove my foot directly into my mouth. "Ezra." I finally manage. "You kept mentioning Ezra, so I thought—"

"You think that just because I mention some guy it means that I'm automatically dating him?" Her hands are on her hips now, her anger still bright, fiery, and more than a little terrifying.

God, if I could take back the last few moments and let my paranoia stay just that, I'd be the luckiest guy in the world.

"Ezra is my ex-boyfriend. He's an obnoxious, sniveling little baby who owns about thirty pairs of various skintight leather pants and has an obsessive fear of them ripping while he's on stage at venues he pays to let him and his mediocre band perform. I am in no way, shape, or form *with* him," she finishes.

I swallow. "Sorry I was just being . . . " I struggle to find a word that isn't "jealous." " . . . a jerk."

"Yeah, you were, now why'd you grab my hand earlier?" she snaps and I startle again. "Why'd you try to fight my battle with Margo for me? Did I look that pathetic to you? Like some little kid who needed some stupid cop to take the lead?" she adds. This time she sounds less angry and more hurt, and somehow that alone makes me feel even worse.

"No . . . that's not . . . " But wasn't that why, at first? I'd looked at her and felt like it was my job to protect her. So instead I say, "You keep wanting to know why I became a cop so young and I told you it was because of my dad. Well, as you figured out before, that's not entirely the truth. I became a cop because of my mom. I wanted to protect her— not myself—from my dad. So I became the one thing he feared—the one thing he was too afraid of being himself. I became a cop. That way if he ever tries anything, if one day he decides that my mother deserves the same pain that he feels, I'll be ready. So that's why I do that. That's why I'm so strict about being a cop and wanted to grab your hand earlier.

That's why. But to be honest . . . " The words seem stuck in my throat, but I've already started. It's too late to stop. "You're the strongest person I've ever met. I wanted to be a cop because I wanted to feel capable—but you're like that all on your own. You're right, I don't know you well, but I know at least that much. And when I grabbed your hand, it was less for you and more for me. Because I needed it; I needed you."

My words stretch across the silence between us and for a moment we stand there, words seemingly failing both of us. The look in her eyes tells me that the hurt is gone, that instead something else is filling her right now.

"Will," she opens her mouth to speak when we hear the loud sound of clapping hands. We turn to look at everyone in the camp. They're all circled around Margo.

"You see this storm? That's on them—that's their punishment. That's Mother Earth trying to get rid of them all. Pretty soon, we're gonna be the only ones

left. Pretty soon, the world will be as it should be."
Margo lets out a deep, riotous laugh, completely at
odds with the cold demeanor she'd shown us earlier.
The camp claps with her, and out of instinct, out of
fear, or maybe out of my own sheer stupidity, I reach
through the space next to me and hold my hand out
toward Sydney's again. She clasps it in hers and this
time she does not let go.

# CHAPTER 11

## *Sydney*

**M**Y MIND IS A WHIRL OF THOUGHTS AND crazy, crazy, crazy, crazy. We need to leave. Now. We need to find Sammy and leave now. These people are not right. Even if some of why they left the surface seems plausible, the way they speak, the way they think, is just . . . wrong.

But Will's holding my hand. And in my head right now, I'm trying to act like it's not a big deal, like guys grab my hand all the time. Like his holding my hand is the last thing I'm thinking about. Because what Margo is spewing out into the fire and into the minds of this camp—into the mind of young Jaime—is what's scary. That's what's important.

Still, Will—Officer Will? Or just Will?—he's holding my hand. And not because he thinks I'm some little girl who needs it, but because he needs me. Because he needs me to stay tough for him.

Syd. He calls me Syd.

I don't know how to feel, but I don't let go. I don't think I even know how to.

"We have to leave this place. Now, Syd." There it is again. Syd. It takes everything in me to focus on his words and not the warmth emanating from his callused hand in mine. Because despite the chaos, despite my fear, despite that he stupidly thought I was still dating a jerk like Ezra, this moment with his hand in mine is perfect.

"I know. But Sammy . . . we need their help. To find Sammy and to find an exit." And it's true. If anyone knows anything about finding a way out, it's these people.

But how can we stay here with them,

knowing that they think our way of life is backwards? Knowing that they're rejoicing over this storm that's turned our lives into chaos? Who knows what's even left of the surface? Who knows if anything that used to matter to us even still exists?

"We'll find him, don't worry. We will." He rubs his thumb over my knuckles and warmth from his hand spreads to the rest of my body.

"Yes, you will," a voice interrupts. I turn to find Margo staring at us with her intelligent eyes. Has she been here all along, listening to our entire conversation? I glare at her. Something about her hasn't sat right with me since the moment I met her.

"And how do you know?" I ask because the insolent side of me can't help it.

She gives a light smile. "Forgive me for earlier. I'd spoken out of turn. We don't meet many people from the surface here. Seeing you here—especially seeing a police officer here—has set me a little on edge."

Well, that's understandable. What they are doing

is illegal and Will is the kind of person who follows rules. The fact that he hasn't slammed handcuffs on them already is testament to how much he wants to find Sammy. How much he wants to help me.

"It's okay," I say.

Margo smiles again and I fight the urge to tell her to get to the point already. "I have something for you. Something that might help you find your brother." She reaches into the pocket of her large sweater and holds out a piece of yellowing paper covered in black and red marks.

"What's this?" Will asks.

"A map of this entire subway system. Not just the train line, but every nook and cranny. Every construction site, every ghost track, every level, and tiny door in this place.

I gape at her.

"H-how did you . . . "

"We made it. My camp and I have been around this entire system hundreds of times. We know our way around this place better than the ones who built it."

Will and I stare down at the piece of paper in her hands. She wasn't kidding. This is everything I could possibly want right now. Sammy feels like a breath away.

"Exits," Will says. "You guys know all the exits. I wish we had thought to ask you sooner."

I shoot him a look. I want to get out of here as much as he does, but not until we find Sammy. I know at first he was reluctant. I mean, I'm not stupid. The guy looked for an exit every chance he got. Part of me—no, all of me—hoped that he no longer felt that way. I hoped that we were in this together.

"The storm has most likely ended," Margo says. "Perhaps you should go to your people and ask for a rescue team to come find him."

Will seems to nod, almost as if he thinks this is a good idea. The hand that he held earlier burns.

Anger surges through me, but before I can

unleash it my mind pauses for a moment, just to think. As much as it hurts me to consider this, Margo is right. Going back is the best option. Will and I haven't bathed or eaten anything substantial in almost two days. And our skills at finding Sammy are abysmal at best. Wouldn't a professional team be better suited to get him? But Sammy only responds to me. If he hears other people calling his name, that could make him hide in an even tighter corner, an even smaller cranny. I'm not sure what to do. All I know is that this isn't working, that we need to find Sammy soon. By tomorrow, he'll probably have finished the last of his Sammy Snacks.

"What do you think, Syd?" asks Will. His eyes implore me and I silently thank him for letting me make the decision. For being on my side no matter what I choose.

"It's a good idea," I slowly nod. "Thanks, Margo. That was kind of you." She smiles and the icily polite veneer of hers begin to melt. Perhaps if I hadn't heard their hate-filled rhetoric only moments ago I would have sided more with these people. Perhaps we would have even gotten along.

"We'll leave now," I say and rush to move toward the purse I left on the ground—completely out of place with the people in Ruiz and Margo's camp. As soon as I take a step in the direction of my things, a wave of dizziness hits me and I nearly stumble over. Will's arms are there to grab me in an instant and I shiver.

"Are you alright?" he asks and I let out a deep yawn.

"I'm fine, I'm just—" I yawn again.

"You must be exhausted," Margo finishes for me. "I doubt you guys have gotten much sleep, especially as you looked for your brother. Why don't you take some time to nap for a few hours? We have cots and warm blankets."

Warm blankets are the last thing I need in the humid air of the subway, but the thought somehow feels welcoming.

"That sounds nice," Will says as he lets out a yawn himself. "I hadn't realized how tired I was."

Margo smiles. "You guys should head to bed, then. I know how tired you are. Here, I'll lead the way."

Just a few hour's rest—then home. Then Sammy. Everything will be okay.

With a lantern in her hand, Margo leads us toward a gutted train car with a small tent made of red gossamer and cloth, tucked just inside. She hands us blankets and pillows as we shuffle ourselves in, two cots laid side by side taking up the entirety of the space.

"Here you are," says Margo. "I'll try to wake you in a few hours, okay? You'll find him—there's nothing to be afraid of in these tunnels."

"Except the dark," Will murmurs in a sleep-addled voice.

Margo puts her hands on her hips.

"Do you remember being a child? Hiding under the covers away from something that scared you?

All the dark really is is the world under a blanket. Comforting, warm, secure. It's the light that really scares people—everything you are, laid out in the open, under a microscope. Darkness just gives you the courage to be your most natural self—to live like no one is watching."

Her voice is comforting, soothing, and it makes a surprising amount of sense. There is something comforting about the steadiness of night, the absoluteness of the dark. It makes everything less real, yet more so, all at the same time.

Margo leaves and takes the lantern with her, leaving us in the dark, almost as if she planned this conversation all along.

"Are you afraid?" I ask Will softly, my words sounding far away in my ears.

"Of what?"

"The dark."

"No." Will pauses. "She was right. There's nothing to be afraid of here."

She was more than right, but I will myself to stay

quiet and lie in my bed, letting the darkness wash over me, hoping and waiting for sleep.

"Hey, Will?" I say, before I drift off, wanting to speak to him before we see each other on the other side of this day.

"Yeah?"

"I think we just ate rats."

He bursts out laughing and pretty soon I'm laughing too and the world around us doesn't seem quite as scary. It's almost like a strange mixture of light and dark—his laugh, this empty train car.

"You gotta admit, it tasted surprisingly good. It reminded me of my ma's Sunday chicken."

"Ew, gross," I laugh and turn onto my side to face him. We pause for a moment, I can feel his eyes on me, but I can't see them. "What you did . . . becoming a cop for your mom . . . being her shield like that? It's brave." I hear his cot creak in the dark.

"What you're doing now for Sammy is brave."

We're silent for so long that I start to think he's asleep and my own eyelids grow heavy.

"Sydney?" he asks and I murmur back a reply.

"Why is it just you? Your mom works and your dad is gone, I get that. Still, why is all of this on your shoulders?"

I breathe out a steady breath, awake again. "My dad used to be my whole world," I say so softly I barely even hear my own voice. "I thought that he'd always be there for me and Sams. My mom worked all night and slept all day, so she wasn't around much, still isn't. Maybe because she doesn't want to be. But my dad had been there. He wasn't much for being mushy and calling me his baby girl or anything like that, but neither was I. We played baseball together, we went swimming at Bergen Beach. He was my best friend—and he knew Sammy better than anyone. He could get the kid to stop crying in less than a minute flat. And when he left, he told me to watch out for him—to be the dad that he didn't want to be. He told me to stay tough. And I promised him that I would."

It sounds pathetic now that I've said it aloud.

Me being there for Sammy because of some promise I made to my deadbeat father. Like the way Will's father shaped him into a cop, my father's actions shaped me into this. A girl too afraid to lose her little brother—the only thing she has left in the world. "It's dumb," I add.

"No, it's not," he says softly. "Your father shouldn't have left you—he shouldn't have placed all that on your shoulders. But what he did? Telling you to be strong? That's made you into the girl you are. A girl who'd beat up a cop and run down subway tracks just to save her brother. The kind of person other people get strength from."

I feel like the world has either fallen away, or pieced itself together. I can't quite tell.

I turn over in my cot and face away from him.

"But it's my fault." I choke on the words as they slip past my lips. "He's gone and it's my fault." I tell him everything. About the concert yesterday, about Ezra and the redhead he kissed at the cafe, about the incredible anger I felt, and losing Sammy because of that.

"Syd, don't say that."

"But it's true! I was so pissed about Ezra and I hadn't even liked him that much, I didn't even really care. And yet I was so pissed that when Sammy was having the biggest freak-out of his life, I didn't pay attention. I was so angry at this guy who means nothing to me that I let my brother run away. Maybe Margo was right—maybe I was the one who pushed him away."

Suddenly, I hear him move from his cot and onto mine. He takes a seat beside me, his hand dropping onto my shoulder.

"You can't beat yourself up over nothing. You can't always be the adult. You're a person, too. It's okay to have a life, to have friends, to have boyfriend struggles. It's okay to have a life outside of Sammy."

I feel my lip quiver despite myself and I'm glad for the darkness. I'm glad that he can't see me cry.

But Will—somehow, some way—hears me anyway, sees me even through the darkness.

"It's okay if you don't, too. It's okay if you don't know who you are outside of Sammy. It's okay to be a little broken, a little lost," he continues.

I wonder how he guessed how alone I feel. That even in school I seem to barely exist. That friends I make are only in passing, the people I speak to don't really see me. My ambitions, my goals all seem to revolve around Sammy. Feeding him, planning for him, and making sure he's okay.

"And what about you?" I ask softly, not because I want to bait him, but because I really want to know. "What's your life outside of being a cop? Outside of the strict code of cop rules that you live by?"

His fingers curl around my shoulders, more comforting than anything I've ever known.

"I don't know," he says quietly before getting up to sit on his own cot.

Impossibly—or perhaps very possibly due to the fact that he's here next to me and feeling the same things that I feel—a smile forms on my lips. "That's okay because neither do I," I add, waiting for sleep to find me.

# CHAPTER 12

*Will*

I DREAM OF WATER AND RAIN AND ELECTRICITY. Of tunnels and darkness and the taste of my mother's Sunday chicken. My father's cigarette sizzling lazily on the arm of his chair. The heavy weight of the gun at my hip. The sound of Sydney's boisterous laugh.

And when I wake from this surprisingly deep sleep, I feel calmer than I have in so long. I almost think I'm home on a Saturday morning, before the academy, before everything. Before my father got shot. Back when everything was okay. That thought quickly ends as I look around and, instead of being greeted by sunlight flooding through my windows, I'm greeted by darkness. But I can also hear the soft breathing of someone beside me which is . . . new.

I check my watch and nearly startle. It's almost noon. Dear God, we've been sleeping for hours— nearly twelve. Margo was supposed to wake us up. We were only supposed to take an hour or so nap. But why had I been this tired? What had happened? I pat my hands against my body on instinct, and finally I notice.

My gun. The gun at my hip is gone.

"Sydney!" I hiss and shake her awake. She squirms and murmurs, but I persist and finally she opens her eyes.

"My gun is missing. It's almost noon. Margo was supposed to wake us up hours ago and my gun is missing."

I see Sydney's eyes whirl as she tries to process this. "You think Margo took it?"

"I think she drugged us, too," I whisper and I put my fingers to my lips to motion for her to do the same. Who knows if they have someone listening in on us—who knows if this is just Margo; maybe they're all in on it.

Sydney's eyes widen. It all make sense—how tired we were last night, how easy it was for her to get us to abandon our mission. I wouldn't have slept this long; I would never have gone to sleep at all, especially since we were so close to finding Sammy.

"All along, this entire time, she's been up to something. I would say I didn't see this coming, but that would be a lie," she whispers.

I nod. "I had a feeling too. It was obvious how much she disliked us. But this? She's trying to get something from us. Or she's trying to hide something."

"What about Ruiz? Do you think he's in on it, too, whatever it is Margo is planning?"

Where Ruiz had seemed nice, Margo had seemed cold and unwelcoming. But they both ruled this camp, they shared a son, and I'd seen the way he whispered into her ear at the end of the night, how close they seemed.

"It's hard to tell," I answer.

"And Jaime?" Sydney asks, her voice small. I hesitate. I know how much he reminded her of Sammy and how much she feels for the little boy.

"He might know something about it, but I find it hard to believe they'd let a little kid in on all of this."

Sydney and I share a look. Margo and Ruiz seemed exactly like the kind of parents who'd include their young son on these kinds of plans in hopes of brainwashing him.

"We should ask him and make him tell us what he knows," says Sydney, with a steely resolve in her voice that makes me look up at her.

"Are you sure?"

"If it means getting Sammy back, I'll do anything."

Because that's it, isn't it? That's what it must all add up to—Sammy. They had his rain jacket, they claimed they may have seen him. They know this system better than most New Yorkers know their own neighborhoods. They have to know something about Sammy—anything.

I nod and together we make our way out of the train car. The camp around us is silent and I wonder if they all knew this was coming. If they laughed with us and told jokes just to make us feel safe, just to make us think they weren't a threat. I want to shout for someone to tell us what's going on, to help us get back to the surface, but it's clear that no one is here. I picture Margo—her cold, hard voice spitting out words filled with venom. Maybe we should have seen this coming all along.

I put my hand on my hip, expecting to feel the familiar weight and shape of my gun, but I remember that it's gone. A part of me expects to feel empty—lost without it. Because this uniform is all I am. All I've been striving for since the moment my father came home drunk and miserable. Since the moment I saw his eyes fall on mine with a challenge. I should feel incomplete, I should feel defenseless.

Especially here, in a place where the sun doesn't shine. But I don't. I can't.

Even without my gun, even here, somehow I feel like there isn't anything I can't do.

I look at Sydney to the left of me, her face molded into a mask of fearlessness and determination. Except it's not a mask or a shield the way my uniform was.

I study her and find that it isn't difficult to do the same, to follow her example, to let her strength become mine.

We walk through the deep tunnels as if the world isn't falling apart.

- - -

"Jaime?" Sydney shouts as we continue along one of the paths Ruiz and Margo showed us yesterday.

"Are you there?" I shout in tandem, making my voice just as kind as hers. We've been looking for the boy for the last half hour. Part of me wants to just try and find his parents and then Sammy—but that's probably impossible, especially without help. And we both remember Jaime talking about how much he loves playing on these tracks—especially when his parents are busy.

So we continue to look through the ghost tracks, rainwater dripping lazily down on our heads, and finally we spot a purple jacket hunched over in the corner. I hear Sydney's breath hitch and I wonder if for a moment she thinks it's Sammy, but she breaks into a jog and cries Jaime's name.

He turns, a soft smile appearing on his face.

"Hey, kid," I say when I catch up, trying my best not to watch him warily as he plays with old action figures along the metal of the track. "Do you know where your parents are?"

The smile on his face falls and he looks between the two of us in fear. No—not quite fear—nervousness.

"I-I-I haven't seen them since this morning."

"Jaime. Remember, I'm a cop. You can't lie to me." And of course I've said exactly the wrong thing.

Jaime retreats farther into the corner, his eyes widened with fear.

"It's okay, Jaime." Sydney speaks up, a smile wide on her face. "I'm your friend, and I promise no one's going to hurt you or be upset with you if you tell me where your parents are." She holds her hand out to him and within moments he latches onto it, his small hands wrapped around hers.

"You promise?" he asks, his voice small and broken. I turn to look at Sydney, watching the indecision in her eyes. There's no way she can keep this promise and she knows it.

"Yeah," she says anyway. "I promise."

We follow Jaime along the ghost tracks, doing our best to not make a sound as we plod down an unfamiliar path.

And suddenly the tracks stop, the tunnels around us begin to narrow, and in front of us is a darkness so all-encompassing even the flashlight in my hand can barely light the way.

"They're down there." Jaime points a finger

toward the passageway. "There in the truction place."

Sydney and I share a look.

"Truction?" Sydney asks, kneeling on the ground to get a better look at him. She holds onto his small shoulders. "What do you mean?"

"The place where all the noise comes from."

Sydney looks up at me questioningly and suddenly I know what he's talking about. "Construction site," I mouth to her and she nods. That's where this passageway must lead—the Second Avenue construction. If I think about it, we've been walking along it for the last few days.

"Are you sure that's where your parents are?"

"Yeah," says Jaime. "And that little boy."

The world seems to pause on a moment—a quick breath of air. I see Sydney trembling, her slim shoulders shaking.

Her voice breaks. "A l-little boy?" She bites her lip and I move to put a hand on her shoulder, mirroring hers on Jaime's. "Blond hair? Blue eyes? A little s-small?"

Jaime nods. "Momma told me not to tell you, but I like you and I don't want you to be sad."

Sydney stumbles into him, wrapping her arms so tightly around him that I'm surprised he doesn't fall over.

"Thanks, Jaime," she says, pulling back to wipe her eyes. "I'll never forget this, I promise." And this time, I can tell she means it. "Now go back, you don't belong here."

# CHAPTER 13

*Sydney*

"**P**APA WILL KILL YOU," JAIME SAYS QUI-
etly. A chill goes down my spine. I can't tell if
he's serious or not, but the knowledge that Ruiz and
Margo have Will's gun is enough to make me pause.

"Jaime, what do you mean that your father will
kill us?"

"Papa doesn't like when people bother him. If I
come with you maybe he won't get so mad."

I can't risk it. I can't risk him getting hurt, especially when Sammy's life is already on the line.

"We need your help back in the camp, Jaime.
Why don't you stay there until we get back? That

way if Sammy comes back, you'll be able to help him." I make my voice strong, but friendly—so there's no room to argue.

He nods, his face serious like this is a game of General and I'm giving him orders. He runs off without looking back and I take a deep, shuddering breath.

"Okay, Will. You heard Jaime—Sammy's close. Let's—" My words break apart when Will suddenly bends in front of me.

"What are you . . . " I start to say, but he doesn't get up, or even look at me. Instead, he grabs onto the laces of my boots and begins to tighten them, tying them in a simple loop. Finally, when he's done, his hazel eyes flick upward and catch mine, his body still kneeling in front of me, like a knight swearing allegiance.

"Now you're ready. Let's bring your brother home."

- - -

Maybe it's the adrenaline, or the fact that we've been here for just about as long as we can stand, but we move through the tracks without a sound. Our feet are in sync. Our rhythm, our pace, even our breaths come out in perfect unity and we move through the maze of the ghost tracks using the map that Margo has given us. We thought it was wrong at first, believing that she'd trip us up to get us lost. But Jaime assured us that it's correct. She must have thought that we'd just give up and go home. She must not have realized that I'd die down here before letting her have Sammy.

"Sydney, over here!" Will shouts from beside me, grabbing my hand and leading us through a dark and narrow hallway. The map in his hand shakes as we continue down the path, a construction site looming before us. There are saws and electrical equipment abandoned and left in a rush, all under a foot or so of water.

"Be careful," he says, pushing us both toward the wall, guiding us on a small foot-wide platform. "It's a tight fit, but all those electrical wires in this water . . . It's not a good mix."

I look over as I try to balance on the tiny ledge, and he's right . . . it isn't a good mix. I'm sure the power has long since been shut down in preparation for this storm. But it's always better to be safe than sorry. I reach for Will in front of me and steady myself with a hand on his shoulder.

Anything could happen down here.

A light from the ceiling could fall and knock me out cold. I could get trapped beneath layers and layers of water. A thousands bolts of electricity could reach inside my system and shake.

Or even worse, even more frightening, the darkness could grab me so thoroughly, so entirely, that I forget to breathe—that I forget who I am. I wonder if that's what happened to Margo and Ruiz. I wonder if they're trying to do that to my Sammy.

"How much of what Margo and Ruiz believe is right?" I ask as we carefully inch our way along the ledge—one foot in front of the other.

"Sydney," he says, his voice stern, and I can almost see the brightness of his badge here in this tunnel.

"No, I'm serious. You can't decide to live like this, scared for your life every other moment of the day and call it paradise. There must be something to what they're saying. Something that rings true." *Because I don't believe they could just do this to my Sams without a reason.*

"They're crazy, Syd! That's the only reason they'd live down here. That's the only reason they'd kidnap a little kid."

I feel like I've tripped one of the wires. That's how badly I shake. I put both hands on Will's shoulders. "B-but you see, Sam's not like other kids. What if he likes it down here? What if he wants to stay? What if he won't come with me 'cause he hates it up there so much and—"

Will stops. He doesn't turn, he can't turn—not when the ledge we stand on is so small. But he pauses, and in the moments that we stay silent, the world seems to turn beneath my feet. He reaches up his hands to grasp mine on his shoulders and squeezes.

"Sydney," he starts, when I begin to catch my breath. "I—" but I don't get to hear what he says next because a sound, louder than anything I've heard since I've been here, fills the air.

A sound. Just a sound. A cry in the distance.

But it's everything.

"Sammy," I breathe out, and Will's body reacts beneath my fingers. It's Sammy. I would know that cry anywhere. It's one of frustration, anger, annoyance—fear that the world is too big to understand. It's when I don't cook the eggs in the yellow pan. It's when I don't sing him the lullaby he wants. It's when the library doesn't have his favorite book.

It's him.

I push past Will and step off the ledge, racing through water and wires toward the sound of that cry.

I hear it again and my heart races.

He's hurting. He's somewhere and he's hurting.

"Sydney!" Will shouts, yelling for me to slow down. But I can't, not when he's so close, not when I hear him in pain.

I run with Will at my heels toward the sound and eventually the tunnel opens up. Large wooden construction panels are posted like barricades across a clearing.

I hear it again—Sammy's voice—and I push past the barricade and long-forgotten construction site until I see him. I don't think I've ever been this relieved in my life.

It's like the world's gotten lighter, my heart even more so. A soft lantern illuminates him, sitting alone in the middle of all this rubble and water and electricity. Same tawny hair, same olive skin, and dark blue eyes, a brown blanket covering his thin shoulders.

"Sammy!" I call his name and his eyes dart toward me—always acute, always aware. It's then that I realize that he's not alone, that Margo is behind him, holding up a can of the warm beans we ate yesterday.

"It's lunchtime!" she keeps saying over and over again to get him to eat. Except Sammy doesn't eat at scheduled meals, that's why he's got Sammy Snacks. The pressure she's putting on him is probably too much.

Finally Margo looks at me, too—watches me with the can of beans in her hands, her eyes just as venomous and untrusting as they were when we first met.

I start toward her, Will at my side, energy pulsing through me. *Sammy's here. Sammy's here. Sammy's here.*

Though before I can even take a step forward, a gun clicks from behind me.

"Don't move, Sydney." Ruiz lets out a wicked laugh. "You too, officer."

# CHAPTER 14

*Will*

I F I WERE ALONE, I WOULDN'T HAVE HESI-
tated. I would have assessed the area, grabbed
Sammy, and put Ruiz and Margo on the ground
before they even had a chance to counterstrike. But
Sydney. Crazy, foolish Sydney.

Running as soon as she heard her brother's cry.

Not stopping to think, not stopping to look—just
running in headlong.

Stupidly brave Sydney.

I had no choice. I followed her, helpless, just as
always.

We ran forward until we finally saw him—well,

Sydney saw him. The first person I saw was Margo, with her dissatisfied frown and her upturned nose. The next thing was stars.

After Ruiz took out his gun, he did what I would do—take out the biggest threat. He slams the butt of the gun hard into my skull and I collapse. Lights fly past my eyes and the pain is incredible. I can hear Sydney screech in anger above me and a wicked laugh from Ruiz that I've never heard before now.

I have to help her—I have to help Sammy. So I stand. Even as my head spins and blood drips from behind my ears, I stand. I almost lose my footing, but Sydney puts an arm around my waist and I let myself lean on her.

Ruiz looks between the two of us, me about to fall over, Sydney carrying me, and smirks. "Did you guys really think you could come down here and take what's ours?"

He speaks the question with more malice than I expected. I hadn't fully believed Ruiz was the brains behind all of this—he'd seemed so much milder mannered than Margo. But this was the real him, the man holding the gun to our heads. The man Jaime said would kill us if he got the chance.

"Yours?" Sydney bites back with twice as much venom. "What makes you think he's yours? He's my little brother and he doesn't belong here. He belongs with me."

"Really, Sydney?" Another voice cuts in from behind us. Margo. "Is that really what you think?" I feel Sydney waver beside me. "Because you've been here for a little over five minutes now and not once has Sammy said your name. Not once has he reached for you."

"Sammy's not like other kids," Sydney says, gritting her teeth. "Sammy has—"

"Asperger's?" Ruiz cuts in. "We know. A boy like that doesn't belong on the surface. A boy like that can't survive. Don't ruin him any further by making him stay up there."

I feel Sydney shake beside me, but her voice still

comes out strong and unwavering. "Why? Why are you doing this? What do you want from us?"

"We want nothing from you," Margo says, this time coming forward to stand beside her husband, Sammy in front of her like a shield. "We just want to protect Sammy. Do you know where I found him? Do you? Of course you don't. It was probably within the first hour he went missing. He was in a drainage hole—a drainage hole in the middle of this hurricane. He could have drowned, all because he was hiding from the sounds of the rushing of people that were too much for him."

"Too much, too much, too much," Sammy says by her side, covering tiny hands over his ears. "Did you know most humans can only withstand up to twenty thousand hertz of sound? I think maybe I can only stand less than that," the little boy says and Margo squeezes his shoulder.

"Sams," Sydney's voice breaks as she pleads with him. If Sammy has any idea what kind of danger he's in, he doesn't let it show.

"You did good, Margo," I say, wincing against the pain in my head, in an effort to calm her down. With someone like Margo, you can never be sure if it will work or not. "Saving Sammy's life like that."

"I know I did." Her eyes flicker toward me. "And normally I would have saved him and left him for the surface police to deal with. We were just going to give him shelter until the storm passed and lead him back toward the surface. But it's killing him, that place. He'll be dead before his next birthday."

"STOP!" Sydney screams violently, about to fling herself at Margo and Margo's holier-than-thou demeanor. But Ruiz waves the gun in our faces again and she falls back.

"Don't deny the truth, Sydney. You're simply not equipped to take care of him. Letting a boy with Asperger's run through the subway alone? What kind of human being does that?"

"What kind of human being waves a gun in front of a seven-year-old?" I spit back, but Ruiz just smiles.

It's like everything about this place is backwards and Sydney and I can barely find our footing.

"Come on, Sydney," Margo starts up again. "You know Sammy would be better off with us. I saw the way you acted at camp—like you knew what was best for Sammy, but do you? Can't you see how much he suffers up there?"

I turn and look at Sydney. Her mind is turning what Margo's just said over and over again. It's wrong—all of it. She can't possibly believe any of what they said. But I can see her losing confidence. Her arm at my waist starts to go slack.

"Hey, Margo. Shut the hell up." Everyone turns to look at me, eyes wide. Even little Sammy with his hands covering his ears.

"Excuse me?"

"Let's say you're right, that he's suffering up in the real world with the rest of us. He'd still never do well with you. You, a person who doesn't know him. You, a person who doesn't get that Sammy doesn't like the pressure of eating at lunchtime and that he needs a Sammy Snack, not a can of beans."

Sydney's eyes go wide as if she's surprised that I remembered all that, but Margo's entire face grows cold. She takes the gun from Ruiz's hand and holds it steady in front of my face, pushing Sammy behind her.

She stares at us coldly. "And to think, I gave you that map in my last attempt to be kind. I didn't expect you to come here. You should have just taken it and left." She turns to her husband. "Deal with them." And Ruiz steps forward, holding two black blindfolds in his hands.

"Gladly." He smiles. "You guys want to go home—so I'll take you home."

"We're not leaving Sammy here with you maniacs," Sydney says, but Ruiz blindfolds her first as Margo keeps the gun steadily aimed at me. I watch as he pulls out a length of rope to tie her hands behind her back. I have to stop this. I have to. Gun or no gun, if I let them lead us out of here, we'll never find

Sammy again. Sentencing him to live down here, with people who barely know him, is a death sentence within itself.

So I dive toward Margo—moving in a burst of energy that she doesn't see coming. I knock Sammy out of the way as I leap toward her, trying to make a clean dash for the gun. I knock her into a wall and slam her wrist against it. The gun clatters to the ground. Still she fights me, biting my ear hard and dashing for the gun when I howl in pain.

But I knee her hard in the stomach and she doubles over, leaving the gun for me to pick up. Triumphant energy pulses through me as I regain my gun. I point it toward her, ready to grab Sammy and Sydney and run, when I hear a strangled cry.

"Will," Sydney says and I turn back to find Ruiz standing over her with a knife at her throat. "Don't."

# CHAPTER 15

*Sydney*

I WANT TOO MANY THINGS. TOO MANY THINGS to accept this as the end. There so much left to do, so much left to have. And yet Ruiz is pressing a knife to my throat as if none of that matters. As if my life doesn't matter. Will's watching me with eyes as wide as saucers and even Sammy, usually so oblivious to fear, is watching me and Ruiz with a look of distress on his tiny face.

Maybe this is enough—all seventeen years I lived—enough for me to feel okay with giving it all up for Sammy. Well, maybe not okay, but satisfied nonetheless. As if the life that I'd dedicated to him has come full circle.

Maybe Will's right—maybe I should have focused on myself more. Maybe I should have made my mom make all the hard calls, forced her to take some responsibility. Maybe I should have made more friends and not have settled for a boyfriend I didn't even really like. Maybe this isn't my fault. Maybe the world turns on its axis no matter what happens to me here.

"Sydney," Sammy says, his voice deathly serious, gravely firm. "Don't be scared." But hearing his voice is making the fear break through me like a flood. It presses against all sides of my skull until I can't even pretend to think straight.

"Stay tough, Syd," Sammy's voice rings out through the darkness and I grab onto it like a tether. I have no regrets. I don't regret being Sammy's big sister. I don't regret him being my world and I don't regret coming down here to find him.

But that doesn't mean I'm going to take this lying down.

I muster every bit of courage I have in me and push my arms out and back against Ruiz behind me, just like they teach you in self-defense class. And with a grunt, he falls backward. I rush toward Sammy without even thinking about it, my arms covering him and shielding him from whatever's about to happen next.

But there's chaos all around and it's hard keeping Sammy from seeing it all. Still, I hold him tight and don't let go.

Margo takes Will's moment of distraction to pounce on his shoulders and reach for the gun, but he flings her off and keeps his gun steady. But Margo is the least dangerous situation. Not as dangerous as Ruiz, recovering on the ground from where I hit him, picking up his knife, and running toward Sammy and me. Instinctively, I shove Sammy behind me, ready for whatever Ruiz is going to do. I brace for a blow that never comes.

Instead, all I hear is an explosion of sound, a ripple in the universe.

I open my eyes and there's blood covering Ruiz's stomach and Will stands, arm extended, gun in hand.

Another sound I wasn't prepared for cuts through the murmur of Ruiz's pain. Margo screams—loud and ear-piercing—running toward her husband. She gets to him, holds him against her face, and sobs. He's not dead—but he's hurt badly. I'm so grateful Sammy's okay that it's hard for me to even notice anything else.

But Will. I notice Will. Standing next to a pile of untreated metal with soldier-like poise, his arm still extended, the gun still in his grip. I see his fingers tremble and I'm reminded of how young he is. This boy who saved our lives, this boy who risked everything to help me. With Sammy pressed behind me, I reach for him and drag my fingers over the arm not holding a gun.

"Will," I say. "It's okay now. It's all going to be okay."

Slowly he turns to me, hazel eyes bright in the dimness surrounding us. It's hard not to notice how brave he is, how strong he stayed for both my and Sammy's sake. His eyes soften and a single tear falls onto his cheek.

"Sydney."

I grab his hand and squeeze and suddenly I feel better. I can't tell who has lent whom strength.

"Shh. I'm here."

He lowers the gun and carefully puts it back in his holster. And as soon as it's back in place, I hug him and let his arms fall around both Sammy and me. It's the most peaceful I've felt in God knows how long—even before we were trapped in this hellhole.

Margo's sobs and Ruiz's grunts of pain break through the silence.

"Leave!" she screams, and when we look back at her we find that her hands and face are covered in his blood. She looks like a horror movie come to life.

"Leave now! And never come back. Do you hear me? Never come back, you hateful, hateful people!" The pain in her voice is palpable and, without another word, we do as she says. We leave, without any intention of ever coming back.

# CHAPTER 16

*Will*

**M**ANHATTAN IS NOT THE SAME PLACE IT
was when we left it. There are no rushing cars,
no hurried pedestrians, no open storefronts and wide
city streets. Instead there is water—seas and oceans
of water.

We'd managed to follow the map Margo had
given us to the nearest exit, a manhole in the middle
of Second Avenue, just a stone's throw away from
Bryant Park and Grand Central. And once we
climbed through, we knew life would not be the
same, even though the storm had passed and the
city around us was now quiet and calm. Still, it is

haunting, seeing a place that was once so vibrant with life, empty and devoid of the people who made it whole.

I look over at Sydney now, as we huddle together inside a cafe with broken doors and windows—empty of even a barista. I've just called for backup and at least the landline in this cafe is working, because without the police, Ruiz would be dead. He would ultimately be fine; the police would come and take him to the hospital, where they would put him back together.

But would we be fine? Sydney and I—the rest of this newfound world?

In the background, the wall-mounted TV plays CNN on a loop of carnage and disaster. Primped and pressed reporters stand in front of overturned cars and broken street signs in areas like the one we're in now—completely evacuated, the residents in storm shelters scattered across the boroughs.

"This storm . . . it wasn't a joke," Sydney says, her eyes taking in everything around us. It hadn't been a joke. Hurricane Angelica had come with a vengeance, raging for two days before it ended, leaving only water and upheaval behind.

Sydney stands and starts making two cups of coffee, Sammy stuck to her side like glue.

"Should I warm up some of these muffins? I think the last thing we ate was rat."

I chuckle, a sad smile crossing my face. "I don't have any money."

It's her turn to smile; her laugh cuts through this dreary afternoon. "We don't need money. Look at this place."

And I do. The storm has changed this city in ways we could have never imagined. According to what we've seen so far from the news, the danger has pretty much passed, but people have still been instructed to stay indoors until all the brackish water has been pumped out.

Sydney and I had taken turns calling our mothers, and both were fine and had been inside for more than twenty-four hours, with police delivering emergency kits to residences all over the city. My parents hadn't been in an evacuation zone, but Sydney's mom was stuck at an aunt's house in Rhinebeck. Other than that, they were fine—everything had moved on without us.

Yet everything was different, not just because of this storm—but because we were different. I was different. Even as we spoke on the phone, I wanted to tell my mother everything I'd always wanted to say but never had the courage to. Things seemed easy now and almost small compared to everything else we'd been through. Like telling my mom that we were too good for this—that we didn't have to live this way, in fear of my father, anymore.

For now, it can wait. For now, I want to sit here and take in the scent of warm coffee and the sound of Sydney's laugh as she jokes with her brother.

"Did you know that hurricanes can breed mini ecosystems? Certain organisms just spring up and come alive."

"I didn't, Sammy," I say, reaching out to ruffle his

hair, then hesitating. "Can I?" I ask. The little boy ponders seriously for a moment and Sydney tries to stifle a laugh.

"Okay, but don't mess it up."

I laugh, as if his dust- and dirt-covered hair can get any messier. Sydney and I both reach over to muss up his hair and we smile when our fingers touch.

We hear a ding and spring apart.

"The muffins are ready." She nods her head toward a tray in the toaster oven and moves to get it.

"I'll help," I say and follow her toward the kitchenette, careful not to step on pieces of broken glass. But she pauses by the oven and takes a step toward me, the sun flittering through the dark hair that frames her face.

She puts her hands on my forearms, tiptoeing until her nose is close to mine, the smell of muffins filling the air between us. I lean forward, fingers reaching to curve around her elbows.

We stand together—curved, fitted—and I know

that everything that has happened between us has happened for a reason—the storm, the rain, all the jagged pieces of us laid out in the darkness and brought to light. To be honest, without her I don't know if I can deal with the brokenness of it all—with the wind and rain that destroyed our city and turned our lives into aftermath.

Sydney leans into me and in that is power that I don't yet have on my own. And when she finally kisses me, I breathe in her scent and realize that this is the first breath I've taken since the rain began.